Maryse Meijer

THE SEVENTH MANSION

Maryse Meijer is the author of the story collections *Heart-breaker*, which was one of Electric Literature's 25 Best Short Story Collections of 2016, and *Rag*, which was a *New York Times Book Review* Editors' Choice and a finalist for the Chicago Review of Books Award for Fiction, as well as the novella *Northwood*. She lives in Chicago.

ALSO BY MARYSE MEIJER

THE SEVENTH MANSION

FSG Originals

FARRAR, STRAUS AND GIROUX

New York

THE

SEVENTH

MANSION

MARYSE

MEIJER

FSG Originals
Farrar, Straus and Giroux
120 Broadway, New York 10271

Printed in the United States of America
First edition, 2020

Library of Congress Cataloging-in-Publication Data
Names: Meijer, Maryse, 1982– author.
Title: The seventh mansion : a novel / Maryse Meijer.
Description: First edition. | New York : FSG Originals/Farrar,
    Straus and Giroux, 2020.
Identifiers: LCCN 2020012310 | ISBN 9780374298463 (paperback)
Subjects: LCSH: Psychological fiction. | GSAFD: Bildungsromans.
Classification: LCC PS3613.E4264 S49 2020 | DDC 813/.6—dc23
LC record available at https://lccn.loc.gov/2020012310

Our books may be purchased in bulk for promotional, educational,
or business use. Please contact your local bookseller or the Macmillan
Corporate and Premium Sales Department at 1-800-221-7945, extension
5442, or by e-mail at MacmillanSpecialMarkets@macmillan.com.

www.fsgoriginals.com • www.fsgbooks.com
Follow us on Twitter, Facebook, and Instagram at @fsgoriginals

10 9 8 7 6 5 4 3 2 1

For Danielle

Is it true

the earth is all there is, and the earth does not last?

. . . .

Living brings you to death, there is no other road.

—GALWAY KINNELL, "Lastness"

THE SEVENTH MANSION

You are on the road or parts of you are on the road you are in two pieces. Blood into the ground, into the dirt, boot near your eyes, someone digging. White fur on meat beside you it is also in pieces soaking some of itself back up. Someone will eat that meat but not you, you are waiting for a different mouth, earth blacker beneath the spade, blacker and blacker the deeper down you go. You and your head. You are just a boy. They put the knife in your hand you would not touch the lamb. Not even to save yourself so the dirt goes right on top, shut your face. Blood left on the stones. On their boots. What a splash you made and now this, all of it on you, in you, covering you, the dirt, the smell of it, it will degrade you, shed the flesh from the bone, the eye from its socket, the heart from its nest of rib, packed hard, you didn't make a sound. Not a single sound. Your life flying up against the sky. Oh, my God. And the legs of the lamb are dragged over you and the boots drag over you and the carts and the roads on top of this road many times over no one knows. You are here. A body losing its blood a head untethered a hand bound behind its back. A boy dragging his sword into the woods waiting to be saved trying to save himself

‡

Back to school. Glossy red brick, high ceilings. Fresh beige paint on the doors. Someone flicking a cigarette in Xie's path as he comes up the steps, hood up. The cigarette hits his knee. Little spray of ash. Fucking psycho. He doesn't look to see who said it. Picks up the butt, puts it in the trash. Locks his bike to the rack, the small of his back damp with sweat, too warm for the hoodie but he wears it anyway, every day, the same with his sneakers, no longer white at the toes, canvas showing holes at the sides. Too late to meet with FKK, the girls already in class so he checks his schedule, slides into the back of homeroom. Even the teacher's eyes on him. Ratty pants and black hair and bright white patch on his bag that says *Take Nothing, Leave Everything*. Smell of linoleum, Lysol, chalk. Mountains beyond the windows. The teacher hands out some papers; he doesn't look at them. Knee jumping beneath his desk. Shuffle to another class. Pants falling off hips. Didn't you get enough to eat where you're from. Something wet shoved down the back of his hoodie. Laughter. He goes to the bathroom, shakes raw hamburger from his clothes. Squiggles of meat on the floor. Tiny spot of blood. He scrubs himself with a damp paper towel, picks up the meat, folds it into the trash. Back in class, English, Mr. Matthews again. Xie opens his notebook. Last year he handed in an essay written in pencil: Meat is Murder. Matthews was furious. Why haven't you formatted this per my directions? Long silence. Xie fingering the strap on his bag. Computers are toxic and they waste electricity. Was this acceptable at your school in California? No. Then why would you think it's acceptable here? Xie didn't answer. Well. No college anywhere is going to accept essays written in pencil. Handing the paper back. I'll give you until tomorrow to turn it in according to the format specified in the syllabus. Next time it will be an automatic F. Xie got the F, then another, then another, until his father convinced the school to let Xie turn in handwritten homework, citing some doctor's note from years before that said computer screens made Xie's dyslexia worse. It didn't matter. He cut as much class as he could get away with, reading in the bathroom, sleeping in the grass beneath the bleachers. Doing just enough work to keep from getting expelled but this is new, the cigarette butt, the meat; at worst last year he had been ignored, little cocoon of silence, fuck with no one and no one will fuck with you; but they all know, now, about the summer, about the farm, about Moore. He can still feel the hamburger on his skin, flesh against flesh; he shifts, folding his arm around his notebook, smudged skull beneath his thumb. Crown of leaves. Drop of water against the bone. At lunch he checks his bike: both tires slashed straight through to the rims. Wincing as he rubs his thumb over the torn rubber. Leni jogging up to him. Hey, we missed you this morning, where were you? Late, he says, and she sees the bike, flinches. Holy shit, she says, pink hair cut jagged to her chin, pale lips stretched across her slight overbite as she frowns, looking over his shoulder to see who's watching. Nobody. Do you want to go to the principal? He waves his hand. Nah, it's okay. They make their way to the parking lot. Jo already on the wall, hair shaved at the sides, plaid pants ripped at the thigh, sucking water from a Nalgene bottle as she checks her phone. Hey whores, she says. Leni hoists herself up on the wall, skinny ass next to Jo's heavy one. Someone messed with Xie's bike, Leni says. Jo grunts, unsurprised. I told you, you should've let me drive you. Xie shrugs, leaning against the wall. Eats trail mix from the pocket of his hoodie. They threw meat at me. Jo chokes out a laugh. They *what*? Hamburger, he says. Like, a pound of it. Raw. Faint unhappy smile. Disgusting motherfuckers, Jo mutters, shaking her head. A swig of water. Was it organic, at least? Leni elbows her. It's not funny. Opening a pack of chips, frowning as she chews. I think we should tell someone. Jo snorts. Like anyone gives two shits about his bike. What are they going to do, call the police? We could, Leni insists. Jo rolls her eyes. Xie chews a handful of nuts. Wind blowing his hair into his face. Last year, on his first day, he'd stood in this same place, eating cold oatmeal from a thermos, when they'd walked up to him, Jo's hand out: We're FKK. They never explained the origin or meaning of that name; he thought it might be some dyslexic abbreviation of *fuck*. We saw you reading Frances Lappé, Leni had said. Are you vegan? He'd just nodded, speechless, as they took their places beside him, the same places they occupy now. The mountains gray beyond the lot. Jo rips a peanut butter sandwich into pieces. Gonna rain, she says, eye on the horizon. First fat drop plump on the hood of a white SUV. The bell rings. They slide off the wall. Tuck their trash in the bin. Xie goes up the steps. James Moore's eyes on his back. Big banner on the brick: Welcome Back.

They had parked Jo's car in the lot of an abandoned Waffle House and walked on foot, 1:00 a.m., to the Moore farm. Head to toe in black. Heavy gloves. Knit masks tight and hot on their heads. At the base of the mountains hardly any houses. No light on at the Moores'; easy to slip to the back, skinning beneath the windows. Do they have guns? Leni whispered. Of course they have guns, Jo scoffed, they all have fucking guns. Leni rolling in her lips, half a step back. Looking over her shoulder. Jo stopped at the gate, bolt cutters poised. Look, do you want to do this or what? It was Leni who'd sat in class with James Moore while his uncle gave a presentation about genetics and mink farming, highlighting their own fur production at a facility only fifteen miles from the school; Leni who'd cried while describing the picture of Ryan Moore and his nephew beside a pile of fresh silver pelts; Leni who said they should do something about it. But it was Jo who had thought of this—no petitions, no letters, no protest. Direct action. Do you? Jo asked again. No, I do, Leni said, wiping her mouth on her sleeve. I'm fine. Sorry. Jo glancing at Xie; he looked back, adjusting his gloves, pure acid in his gut. They cut through the chain. Slither of metal against metal. Behind the gate a huge concrete lot covered in straw and shit. God, Leni breathed. Whisper of fur in the dark. Slow steps closer.

The mink curled in mesh-wire cells no more than ten inches wide, stacked on row after row of wooden platforms stretching a hundred feet or more to the back of the farm. They'd seen the aerial maps, had known what to expect, but it stopped them anyway, for a moment, to see in the flesh just how many animals there were. Jo put her hand against the front of a cage; the mink shifted inside, hissing. Smooth shine of eyes. Hi, babies, Jo whispered. We're not here to hurt you. Slow hard press against the metal clips at the top of the box and the door sprang open, nearly hitting her chin. Come on, she said, reaching for the mink, go! The mink hurtled up the arm of her glove before leaping to the ground, scattering straw, claws against concrete. Xie and Leni running, each to the head of a row, snapping back the clips. Even through the gloves you could feel how soft those bodies were. Silver ghosts swarming beneath the gate. Xie's hands so fast on the clips, trying to balance speed against silence. Sneakers slipping on straw, on shit, breath wet in the mask. He couldn't see the girls but he heard them, felt them, moving in the same rhythm, the three of them a single machine. In the last row a mother and her babies, five or six, teeth bared; they would not leave their cage and Xie shook it, hard, trying to rattle them free, stifling a shout as one leapt at his face, the cage rocked free of its stand. He fumbled to right it but it fell, too loud. Fuck. Jo pointing to her watch, eight minutes up, Leni already sprinting to the road and Jo following but at the gate Xie stopped, turning to make sure they'd emptied every row, flashlight jumping in the dark. Faint scent of fur and the most. Beautiful sight. Pockets of night in the open mouths of the cages. The barn a black shadow against the mountains. Breeze stirring the straw. The almost alien sensation of joy: We did it. And then he was down, cheek straight to the concrete, Moore's hard breath in his ear. Don't move, motherfucker. Spit of blood catching in the black hairs of Xie's mask, rattle of air and groan. Pain somewhere in the distance, waiting for him to feel it, but he felt nothing. Run, he thought, closing his eyes. Run. Run.

Jo drives him home. Xie carries the bike to the garage, past his father unloading tools from his truck. Hey, Erik says. What happened? Nothing, Xie replies, leaning the bike against the back wall of the garage. Erik looking at Jo. She shrugs. It was James, had to be. Leni scrubbing at the gravel with the toe of her boot. They threw stuff at him, too, she says, eyes wide. Erik dropping a wrench into a box, loud clatter of metal on metal. Wiping his hands on his jeans. You tell anyone? Xie's jaw tight. Squatting on the step to stitch the long gash in the sidewall of the tire with a piece of dental floss. Finger slipping on the needle. He shakes his head, once. Goddamn it, Erik mutters. He goes inside. Jo and Leni exchange a glance. You want to come over later? Jo asks. Not tonight, Xie says. Okay, well, call us, she says, turning to take Leni's arm as they walk back to the Jetta. Slow roll from the driveway. Inside the house his father's voice rises, falls. Xie drops the needle, makes a knot in the floss. Erik comes back out, hand against the screen behind Xie. They're giving you two options. You can transfer to another school in the district, or you can take a tutor for the semester until things settle down. I have to talk to the principal in the morning and let him know what you decide. Xie scrubs his palms against his thighs. Okay. Silence. Erik scratching the back of his skull. You want me to take a look at it? Jutting his chin toward the bike. No, it's fine. A pause. You know I have to call your mother. Yep, Xie says. I don't have a choice. I said *okay*, Xie replies, sharp. His father slams the screen. Xie on the step, arms around his knees. Rain pouring off the door of the garage. Water splashing the drive. Xie, his father calls. He drags himself inside. Takes the phone, pressing it against the cheek that Moore had smashed against the concrete; it doesn't hurt anymore but he remembers how much it did, hairline fracture and a bruise that distorted half his face for weeks. Now they're kicking you out of *school*? his mother is saying. Because of that stunt you pulled this summer? Xie quiet. Wrapping the phone cord around his wrist. Wrap. Unwrap. They're not kicking me out, he says. Oh, okay, well, if your father didn't think it was necessary to ask them to give you special treatment all the time that's exactly what they would do. You can't just keep running away from the consequences of your actions, Xie. I wasn't trying to, he says. They don't want me there, I don't want to be there, why should I go? Because it's good for you! she yelps. Not everything is about what you want. Think of all the money we're spending, your father isn't exactly wealthy, and we've worked very hard for what we have,

very hard, Jerry is very supportive but he just doesn't understand what's going on with you and frankly neither
do I. You don't have to send anything, Xie says. Of *course*
we do, what are you saying, how else do you expect to
pay them back for all the damage you did? He hears the
chatter of pills on the other end of the line, the sound
of his mother arranging her nightly cornucopia of vitamins on a plate. They didn't even live, she says. They all
got shot or trapped or run over. I mean you didn't really
think any of it through, did you. Xie peels the cuticle
away from his thumb. Do you need to talk to Dad again?
No, she says, suddenly composed, satisfied with this proof
of disaster, a disaster she'd predicted ever since he was
young, predictions his father ignored. I love you, she says.
But I need you to be good. Can you be good? Yes, Xie says.
She hangs up.

He unwraps the cord from his wrist. His father's hand at
his back. I'll make dinner in a minute, Xie says. Just going to take a walk. It's raining, Erik says. I know. Slips out
the back door. Trips over the back step. Curses. Hood up
against the rain but he is soaked in a second. He walks
into the backyard. The remains of summer's strawberry
and zucchini plants sunk in mud, surrounded by weeds,
a mess. He unlatches the gate, slips down the narrow
bank to the stream, which has swelled almost as high as
the log that crosses it. He jogs over the log, careful of the
moss, to the fence, higher than his head. NO TRESPASS-
ING. He rolls back a flap of chain-link, his sleeve catching

on the steel. He faces the trees. Breathes. The woods are
a mile deep, two miles long, bound by the highway at the
east, a local road at the west, the house at the south. To
the north, in the clearing that used to be full of ash and
oak, there is a field of wild grass. It's not dark enough to
see the light yet but it's there. He doesn't know where it
comes from, some building in the clearing; he has never
gone near it. He walks, arm out to touch the trunks as he
passes. The wood is pure birch, *Betula pendula*, not native
to the state, considered invasive in some places, crowding
out slower-growing, longer-living species: trespassers,
like him, creating a screen between Xie and the town,
between Xie and everything else. A mile from any neigh-
bor, twice that to the tiny downtown with its strip malls
and craft shops and bars. He spent every day of his first
summer here. Learned the names of the ferns, the flowers, the birds. Nuthatch. Barn swallow. Goldfinch. He
had found his nest; he had wanted to disappear. Stupid.
To think you could. He pauses at a trunk split in half by
the last storm, its branches grazing the soil. The crown
is still connected to the trunk by an arch of bark chalk-
white on one side, bright yellow on the other, the sap-
wood and heartwood jaggedly exposed at the top of the
break. He tugs a strip of bark from the wound and puts
it in his mouth, chews. Finger deep in the cracked body
of the tree, which is still alive, pumping the last of its
sugars through the wood. A fox slides through the fallen
crown, twitching the leaves aside. Weird nighttime eyes,
rain combing its pelt close to its skinny haunches. Xie
waits, bark bitter in his mouth, as the fox darts back into

the brush. In its wake he sees something white in the juncture of two broken ferns; tiny bones, gently curved, with knobs like fists at either end: femurs. Picked clean. He puts them in the pocket of his hoodie. Walks home.

After dinner his father pulls a pack of cards from the sideboard Xie loves, teak with a satin finish that still shines. All their furniture is like this, simple, Danish, true vintage, inherited from Erik's parents. His father shuffles, hands fast on the cards; he had paid for his wife's engagement ring with the winnings from a single evening of poker. His mother used to say the ring would be his someday. An entire circle of diamonds. For the girl he was supposed to marry. He scoops up the dealt cards. More diamonds. His father frowning as he fans his hand. Shit, he murmurs. They won't talk about the phone call, about school. Snap of plastic against the table. His thumb bleeding from where he pulled flesh away with the cuticle. Sucks it. Let him win. Pretend like you didn't.

Up in the attic before bed. Putting the bones into the brass dish along with the others, six or seven dozen: femurs, vertebrae, ribs, some brown and brittle, others, like tonight's, fresh, a pure dry white. He puts the dish at the head of the mattress, pulls the curtain over the window. The room turns to velvet. Softest black. For a while there isn't anything in his head. The sound of the

creek, the occasional cry of a whip-poor-will, a nightin-
gale. Xie turns on his side. Puts his fingers in the dish.
Imagine. A single white curve. The horizon of a skull
against the velvet. How smooth it would be, if you put
your mouth against it, drew your lips to the crest of the
brow, tongued the deep sockets, inhaled the scent of
the wafer-thin walls of the nasal cavity, more delicately,
numerously chambered than a beating heart. Kissed each
loose tooth. Licked the entire length of the jaw, slowly
bit the arch of the cheek. You imagine everything, as the
void peels away from the body bone by bone: skull, spine,
clavicle, ribs, hips, thighs, knees, shins, feet, you go as
slow as you can. Hands against every hollow, every curve.
How quiet it would be. How quiet it is. Alone with it. You
turn your mouth into the pillow. Lift your knee against
the sheet. Your hips against its hips. Your mouth against
its mouth. Whatever movement might be possible, without hurting it, you'd learn, you'd know, it would tell you,
show you. How it fucks you. How you fuck it. Making
sense of your own flesh. You spread your arm across the
mattress but there is no body to embrace. There never
will be. And you fall straight through the ceiling into
sleep on this thought and even the velvet does not catch
you, you just fall and fall.

He comes downstairs at noon to find Erik at the kitchen
counter, pouring coffee into a thermos. Get dressed.
You're coming with me. Xie pauses in the doorway.
What? To work, Erik says. Why? I don't want you lying

around all day. Xie rubs his brow. Dad, I'm not. Erik cutting him off, grimacing as he swallows his coffee. Just get ready. Fifteen minutes later in the truck, dozing against the glass, news on: ice melting at both poles, whales eating plastic bags, California still on fire. Erik spins the knob. They drive for half an hour and stop at a strip mall, where two other men wait in a gutted office space, ripping up old carpet. They nod, smileless, when Erik introduces them. Xie looks at the floor. You're gonna help me install that, Erik says, pointing to a toilet and sink stacked in a hallway. And we have to take the old stuff out. Xie tucks his chin into the neck of his hoodie. Everything, even the things they have to get rid of, look brand-new. In the bathroom his hand keeps slipping on the wrench. Sweating in gloves several sizes too big. No window. The other men begin laying down carpet pads, each shot with the staple gun echoing down the hall. Dad, Xie says. Dad. Erik grunts beneath the sink. Yeah. I have a blister. Erik frowns. From what? Xie shrugs. Go get a Band-Aid from the truck, Erik says. Xie brushes the dust from his knees, goes outside. Fresh air. Beyond the ugly blunt stucco pine trees feather the horizon, surrounding the university in the hills, a liberal hippie arts school Erik hoped would entice him with its vegan meal plans and social justice majors. But he'd had all that in California; it wasn't different buildings, different people, different schools that he had wanted but something else, something he recognized in the woods as soon as he saw them. Hey, a voice calls, behind him; Xie stops a step shy of the truck. Little sip of air. Hey, I want to talk to you.

Xie looks over his shoulder. A middle-aged man, thick beard, jean jacket, peeling away from the wall of a dough-nut shop. You're that kid, right? That's you? Xie blinks. The guy comes in close, jacket brushing Xie's sleeve. Kid who messed with the Moore place? Going around with your black shit and taking people's property? Xie steps back. They're not property. What'd you say? They're ani-mals, Xie repeats. They're not property. Like hell they're not, you know how much you cost that family? Actually, yeah, I'm paying for it, Xie says. So. Don't really need the lecture. You mean your daddy's paying, the man corrects, finger in Xie's face. Consequences of your actions mean shit to people like you, self-righteous tree-hugging fag-gots. Shut up, Xie whispers. The man grabs the front of his hoodie, yanking Xie into an almost-embrace. Don't fucking mumble when you talk to me. Xie closes his eyes. Thinks of Moore on his back. Breath on the side of his face. The man lets him go with a shove and Xie stumbles, back against the truck. The man spits, turns. You watch yourself, hear. Inside the building the men are unrolling a tarp, perfectly visible through the windows. Xie gets a bandage from the glove compartment, spreads it over the burst blister. When he walks back into the building the men clear their throats. In the bathroom Erik is twisting the new taps into place. What took you so long. Gestur-ing at the gloves. Xie pulls them on, picks up the little bits of junk everywhere: shredded plastic, splinters of wood, loose nails, paint chips. One by one into an empty paint can. When the can is full Xie puts it in the back of the truck, then climbs into the cab. Peels off the sweaty

gloves. Sleeps. When he wakes he sees Erik crossing the
lot, blotting the sweat from his brow as he gets inside the
truck. How's your hand? It's okay. Erik nods, long suck of
his teeth. You want to go back in? No, Xie says. Silence.
A sparrow lands on the hood of the truck, shivers, flies
off. You know I just want things to work, Erik says. Here,
I mean. For you. That's all. Xie gazes from blacktop to
roof to sky. I know, Xie says. Erik rubs his face. They used
to laugh about how Xie's first word was No. For a year
no matter what anyone said Xie would yell, No no no.
If something scared Xie—the noise from the clock or the
car engine or the air conditioner—Erik wanted to show
Xie how it worked. Kneeling beside him, saying, Look.
Trying to prove there was no monster lurking in the machines. But Xie refused to look. Bad, he said about the
air conditioner. Bad the car engine, bad the clock. Erik
insisting, We have to learn to live with these things. Tick
tock. Rumble. Roar. No.

Xie has been to the public library only once, with FKK;
they had gone to find books about animal liberation and
found none. When Leni complained to the librarian he
had told them, We are a general interest facility. Which
made Jo laugh out loud as she smacked a stack of romance
novels. You mean we should be reading this shit instead?
At which point they had been asked to leave. I'm supposed
to be here for a, um, tutor, Xie says, approaching the front
desk. Greg, the librarian, says, Yes, I am aware. Cool gaze
behind his gray glasses. Xie glances around the room;

shallow rows of dark metal shelving, half full, surround a bank of tables with ancient computers, chess games, magazines. A man sits near the water fountain, taking notes from a dictionary. Everything smells like dirty laundry and old glue. In the children's area a woman in a blue jacket waves, a huge yellow sun cut from construction paper stuck to the window behind her head. Xie shifts the strap of his bag over his chest. He could leave. Doesn't. Tugs his jeans up, shuffles to the table. The woman stands, reaching for his hand. Strong grip. Hi, Xie? I'm Karen. Mid-twenties, green eyes, thin strawberry blond hair to her shoulders. Backpack on the desk like a student's, full of folders. He sits, knee jumping beneath the table; he has to think hard to stop it, then it stops. How are you? Karen asks. Fine, he says, looking at the smiley face someone scratched into the tabletop. Good, she says. It's nice to meet you. He glances up, then back down. Karen takes a deep breath. So, we'll be meeting three times a week for three hours to go over the assignments. Sliding him a schedule, pointing with a pen. I have your course books here; we'll discuss the readings and whatever homework the school assigns, which you'll turn in to MacAdams on Fridays. At the end of each month I submit a report about what we've covered here and that's pretty much it. The bathroom's just that way, you can use it whenever you need. And we have a fifteen-minute break around noon. Sound okay? Xie clears his throat. Mm-hm. It looks like you had a bit of a rough time with math last term, she says, consulting one of her folders, so why don't we start with that. She opens a textbook, tucks her hair behind her ears. I was looking at some of your past work and it seems like this is where you get stuck; can you tell me what you're thinking when you get to this point? Watching him repeat the problem. There, she says, gently, you left out a step. The librarian stares; Greg knows, everyone knows, does Karen? She must. That I tried to help them but they died anyway. There you go, she says, nodding at the end of the hour, Xie's pencil worn to the wood. You've got it. Karen puts down her pen, pulls a lunch bag from her backpack. You can't eat in here, Greg calls. Yes, we know, she says. Xie follows her outside. Karen settles on the steps. He hesitates, then sits beside her. Tipping trail mix from the pocket of his hoodie into his hand. Do you live nearby? she asks. Yeah. Near the creek. That's a long walk for you, she says. He shrugs. I don't mind. I like the woods. You have brothers? Sisters? No. Just your parents? My dad. What does he do? He's a, um, contractor. She uncaps a bottle of iced tea, drinks. And you're from California. He squints. Don't you know all this already from a file, or . . . ? She shrugs. Just curious. She peels plastic wrap from a sandwich. Pieces of ham, clotted with mayonnaise, spill from the sides as she lifts it. He grimaces. Why do you eat that. Oh, that's right, she says, almost to herself. You don't eat meat. I don't eat animals, he corrects. I don't know why anyone does. Karen's back stiffens against the step. I'm sorry if it offends you. Silence. Neither of them looks at the other. Sun soaking the steps. Xie rubs his chin on his arm. Rises. Goes back inside to sit at the table, looking at the stacks of folders, books, the paper, the pencils, her green pen. The last time he ate meat he was twelve years old, after the spill: Xie was Alex then. Even miles from the beach, they could smell something off; at first they thought it was the sandwiches, ham pressed hot in the pockets of Erik's windbreaker, but the closer they got to the beach the stronger the smell became, noxious, chemical. They parked at their usual spot, yellow tape blocking access to the beach beyond. A black ribbon flat against the horizon; that was the water. No trace of blue. On the rocks below the lot a half dozen pelicans huddled together. Coated from beak to foot in oil. Don't touch them, his father said. Someone will come help. But there was no one. The black sea lapping the sand. Those bewildered eyes. He watched as one of the birds collapsed, its head twisted sideways against its neck. His father pulled him away. The fire on the water burned for two weeks; the beach remained black for a year. Sea turtles, dolphins, whales, gulls, crabs, otters, fish rolled up by the waves in the tens of thousands. Oil on meat on sand. No stopping it. Xie got headaches, bloody noses; he was always tired, couldn't sleep. His mother standing in the doorway. Stop playing games, you're fine. But his father was never angry. Scared of what he saw. Xie curled in the dark. Unable to make it from one room to another. The people who used to go to the beach just went somewhere else. Life as usual. Slumped in his seat as his father fed gas into the truck he suddenly couldn't stand it. Stopped standing it. He opened the door, started walking. Alex, his father called, but he was not Alex anymore. He poured out all the milk in the house, threw packages of lunch meat to the dogs next door, sold his computer for a bike. When he was thirteen the beaches turned yellow again but he still smelled the oil, still saw the birds collapsing against the rocks. He refused to fill his prescriptions. Chose a new name. A new town. As if he could outrun it. The clock ticks. Karen stays outside, giving him or herself a moment. Xie's knee trembles beneath the table, all the blood in his body pounding. Nowhere to go. He draws a skull in the margin of his homework. Erases it. Presses the tip of his pencil, hard, against his jaw. Two more hours. By the end of the day, three billion animals will be dead. You just sit there.

In the afternoon Jo and Leni are waiting for him in the library parking lot, leaning against the hood of the Jetta, Leni in tight plaid pants and Jo in ripped jeans and a black tank top, hair fully spiked, both of them wearing more eyeliner than Xie can really understand. Hey, he says, Shouldn't you be in school? We called in sick, Jo says. Get in, loser. He climbs into the backseat. Leni leans to look out the windshield as Karen comes down the steps, shading her eyes against the sun. Is that your tutor? Yeah. You like her? She's okay. Too bad she's not hot, Jo says with a smirk. Like he would even notice, Leni says, and Xie shakes his head. Where are we going? he asks. Jo pats coconut oil on her thick lips, smacks them together in the mirror. I've been emailing this guy, Peter, who runs an environmental colloquium at the university, which is kind of a lame crunchy hippie thing, but he told me last week that he *also* runs a secret meetup for radical activists. Invitation only. So we're invited? Xie asks. The girls grin. What do you think?

The meeting is in the basement of a Unitarian church forty-five minutes from town. A couple dozen people wearing Crocs and battered boots, cargo pants, canvas jackets, beanies, leaning against the walls or grouped on folding chairs, drinking beer or tea or cups of kombucha. The room cool, damp, wood paneling on the walls weirdly domestic, like a rec room in some '70s duplex. Xie pushes his hands deep into the pocket of his hoodie. Leni bends to re-strap her boots, shin-high and glossy. Are those new? Yeah. Jo got them for me. They're vegan leather. He elbows Jo. Where's my new boots? She elbows back, hard: In the dumpster along with the rest of your shit. A guy with a bushy red beard and pink cheeks enters from a door on the opposite end of the room, raising a hand in their direction, big smile, small sharp teeth. Hey, wow, thanks for coming out, he says. I'm Peter. You're FKK? Jo nods. Yeah, this is Leni, Xie. Warm hand taking each of theirs in turn. We heard about the action you guys did at the Moore farm, Peter says. Really inspiring. Xie glances at the girls; Jo lifts her cup up, like, cheers. I'm sure Jo already filled you in, but we're an anarchic organization, Peter says. There's no official affiliation, no leadership, though we share a lot of the same values and goals concerning the environment with a lot of the more radical biocentric groups out there. We're here to make connections, share resources, support each other in whatever we're doing. We just ask that you don't talk about what's discussed down here with people who aren't members, so everyone stays safe, okay? They nod. Cool. I'm really stoked for you guys to meet Nova, Peter says. She's going to have a lot to share with us about her work with E.A. Yeah, we can't wait, Leni says, glancing at Xie, who just nods like an idiot. Let me introduce you to some people, Peter says, arm out, and when he and the girls turn toward the rest of the group Xie hesitates, his anxiety as high here as anywhere, even though these are all supposedly people like him, like FKK, people who care about the things he cares about, why can't he enjoy it? Maybe he just. Needs some air, to pee, to get a drink of water, something. He jogs up the stairs, turning down the hall at the top, head down. Running straight into a body. Shit, he breathes, sorry. A girl lifts her head from the water fountain, wiping her mouth on her sleeve. Taller than Xie, a few years older. Dark hair pulled back. A fresh scar on her forehead, bright purple, as thick as a finger, carved from temple to temple. The flesh on Xie's neck prickles. She looks at him, black gaze half blank. Did you need to use this? No, Xie replies. I was just going out for a sec. Oh, she says. Me too. Eyes scanning the wall opposite. Neither of them moves toward the door. If Peter comes out here tell him I just can't, you know, she says. Continuing a thought begun before his arrival, not directed toward him but aware of him, rooting him to the floor. Soft voice. At odds with her wide square face, her thick shoulders. Rocking slightly on the heels of her ballet flats, too big, in fact all of her clothes wrong for her, a white button-down gaping at the chest, black skirt wrinkled, tight, as if borrowed from a friend not quite her size. I mean, does it make sense? At *all*? Sitting in that . . . shitty room with their craft beers like they do every week, so ready to change the system. How? By—what, shopping at the nearest co-op? The people who think they're in charge *love* this shit, okay. They are fucking laughing their asses off every time Peter buys an energy-efficient light bulb. She sticks her arm out, sudden, a packet of crackers in her hand. He flinches. You want this? She smirks. Someone gave me this shit like I want to eat it. Because it's *vegan*. She rolls her eyes. Oh, well, in *that* case I'll eat the whole fucking box, right? Never mind that what it actually *is* is garbage wrapped up in a piece of garbage that I'm supposed to enjoy while we all huddle down there in the dark like a bunch of fucking cockroaches, signing our little petitions begging Mr. So-and-So to please not let the frackers pour poison into our drinking water when the problem, the *problem* is that the idea of clean water in the first place is unimaginable. The environment is always already trashed. You look at a tree and it's garbage and you look at the soil and it's garbage, the air, the water, it's just future garbage, all of it, so who is going to give a shit? Nature is a vacation, it's boring, it doesn't even *exist*. Do you realize that? It's not even fucking *out* there, because no one can see it, and if you see it, I mean if you really think you know what the earth even is, if you think you're a part of it, that you want to serve it instead of destroy it, then you are fucking crazy, okay? You're a ghost trying to save a corpse. She rubs the scar above her eye, grimacing. He tries to say something but she puts her

hand up without looking at him, head down, an exhausted animal listening to its own blood. Two days
ago I saw a man step on a caterpillar, she says. And when
I told him to watch out he looked at me, truly confused,
like, What? And I pointed to the ground and the caterpillar's guts were stuck to his shoe and he still said What.
She shakes her head, narrowing her eyes on the door at
the end of the hall. You can't convince people to see what
isn't there. It's too late. So you might as well just pull a
trigger. She rips the elastic from the bun at the back of
her head, hair tumbling against her collar as she turns
away from the fountain. Wait, he says; but someone is
coming up the stairs, calling her name. Nova smiles at
Xie, furious, eyes bright, before heading for the exit, forearms hard into the crash bar as she spills out into the
night, the black ridge of ash trees pricking the horizon,
crowning her dark head.

They walk to the car, Xie's arms wrapped tight around
his waist, Leni tripping in the gravel, scraping the toe
of her new boot. Damn. Laughing, giddy from the past
two hours, the girls talking at a table with a handful of
other women while Xie listened, exhausted, mute. Peter
outside trying to track Nova down; neither ever returned
to the room. I don't know about you all but I need to get
fucking *high*, Jo says, you want to spend the night? Xie
wanting only to sleep, too tired even to think of walking through the woods, he doesn't say yes or no so they
just drive to her house. Filing into her big white kitchen.

Gleaming concrete counters, a bowl of green apples. Jo reaching into the violet light of the enormous refrigerator, filling her arms with beer. Xie takes an apple from the bowl. Upstairs Jo opens their beers on the lip of her desk, sucks the fizz from each before handing them around. Xie stares at the label on the bottle. Don't worry, it's organic, Jo says, just drink it. The girls on the bed, him on floor, his back against the nightstand. Deep carpet. He puts his hand in it. When he helped his father pull up carpets in California he was always amazed by how much filth lay beneath them. You can't really keep anything clean. He sips the beer. Hates it. Likes it. Jo rolls a joint, careful, Leni trying to help her but Jo elbowing her away. Stop, let me do it. Licking the paper closed, quick zip of her thumb to seal it, twice. Leni lights the joint. Passes it down to Xie. He inhales. Not coughing. Like he's done it before. Bitter, sappy. Jo's low whistle and Leni swatting him on the knee, That's it. Quick swallow of beer. The joint goes around, no one speaking. By the last hit Xie is heavy all over. Tipping the bottle to see what's left, skinny slop at the bottom, drink that too. What'd you guys think, Jo says. Should we go back? For sure, Leni says with a sigh. Everyone's so nice there. I wish we could have met Nova, though. I heard she's a fucking badass. She'll be back, Jo says, leaning to stub out the joint, last exhale from the side of her mouth. Xie gazing at the big window over Jo's bed, ghost of light against the glass from the security beam over the backyard. Leni scoots down the mattress until she is half on top of Jo, leg thrown over her hip. Soft wet sound of their kissing.

Xie can't imagine what it would be like with a girl. With anyone. He doesn't know why. He picks the skin off the apple, eats it. Leni making a sound like being gutted, Jo murmuring, It's okay, slow down, slow down. Xie sucking the juice from the fruit. Sour. Like the beer. Thinking of. That picture. Somewhere. Some book. Of a statue, a skeleton, hip cocked, grinning toward an upraised arm. Holding its own heart in its hand. Set at the head of a tomb of a prince in the 1500s, in France; Xie had never seen anything like it. Sensual, strange, triumphant. He'd thought of bodies like that before but for the first time there was proof, that someone else had thought bones were beautiful, too, he had been, what, eight? Nine? And already afraid of what it meant, to like something like that, to want it, knowing it had to be a secret. Jo breaks off the kiss, sitting up to open another beer. You all right down there? Yeah. His voice hovering somewhere beyond him. Imallright. Jo holding the bottle for Leni, tender. Stroking her hair. Xie on his hands and knees. What are you looking for? Gold, he says, maybe out loud. Leni's laugh smothered in the side of Jo's huge breast. He used to imagine coming home to a body like that prince's. Lacing its fingers between his. How do you explain that. To anyone. He puts his face against the carpet. Almost to the bathroom. Just stand up. Xie. What. Seriously, are you okay? Yeah. Please don't vomit on the carpet. I won't. Promise. I promise. Swear. All three giggling. Pinkie-swear. The girls at his sides, holding his arms, haul him up and to the bathroom. He leans in the doorway, I'm fine. You sure? He nods. They close the door. He opens his fly, hand against the wall, dark blue tile, the closest Jo's parents would let her get to black. The toilet bowl gleams. Everything pristine. The maid comes to clean four times a week. He snorts. Cock in hand. Hates the way it feels, pure flesh, useless. Look in Jo's mirror. Tray of scented soap. You will be sick. You are sick. She said it, didn't she, she looked right at you. Not a judgment, but an exhortation. You can't make people see what they don't want to see but it doesn't mean you have to give up seeing. Finished pissing. Clumsy wipe of the seat. Sit. Sleep here. Head against the wall. It's a body you want. Someone's arms. Around you. That's all. Tears on your face. You don't notice. Night.

Fifteen minutes late. Head down as he approaches Karen and then just sits there. No hello? she says, eyebrows raised. Hi, he mumbles. You want to give me your algebra homework? I, um, don't have it. She presses her lips together, looks away, then back at him. Why not? He shrugs. Sorry. You just didn't get to it or you didn't know what you needed to do, or . . . ? He smooths his hand against his knee. I just, uh. Didn't. Do it. Long silence. He can feel her deciding whether to be angry or let it go, help him or not help him. He pulls out his algebra book. Thinking of what Nova said, about Peter and the others in the basement, like cockroaches, if she thought that was bad what would she think of this, a supreme waste of time, but what choice does he have. Karen leans forward, pencil lifted; they do the homework together. It takes them an entire hour. No, it's wrong, look, check the formula, she says, and he checks it, he tries, paper worn through where he has to erase again and again. Finally he passes the paper to Karen for the last time. Hallelujah, she sighs, sitting back in her chair. Glances at the clock. Could you give me a sec? she says. I need to make a call. He shrugs. Sure. She stands, bumping her thigh into the lip of the table, looking at her phone. Goes outside for five minutes, ten, fifteen; he can see her through the window, pacing around her car before leaning against the door, head down. He waits. A child and its mother stare at him from another table, a box of broken crayons between them; he pretends not to notice. Opens a textbook at random, reads. Karen returns, tapping his shoulder with something wrapped in wax paper. Here, she says. What is it? Peanut butter sandwich. What's in the bread? She snorts. Nothing. Wheat. He looks up at her. Xie, it's vegan, I promise. No corn syrup, all-natural, the whole nine yards. He takes it. Thanks. They sit on the steps. He eats half of the sandwich, slow, picking out a seed from the bread to drop on the concrete for the ants. Chin on his knee. Some girls picked you up the other day. They your friends? Yeah, that's FKK. FKK? It's their—group name, like a thing they started. For animal rights. Ah, Karen says. Compatriots. I guess, he says, watching as the ants surround the seed. What kinds of thing does FKK do? Xie frowns, chin wrinkled against his jeans. Actions. Actions? Like, protests, or signing petitions, writing to

politicians. What kind of protests? Um. Just, against factories and stuff. We did one last year. At the outlet mall.
In Alliance? Yeah, that one. We downloaded these signs
from the PETA website. He shakes his head, remembering. THE PRICE OF YOUR FASHION IS MURDER. Pictures
of cowhides piled in leather factories, rabbits being de-
furred, silkworms poured into vats of boiling water. Jo
screaming through a bullhorn for ten minutes before it
started to rain. They'd stood there for two hours, silent
except for the occasional FUCK YOU from Jo whenever
someone called them idiots or freaks or told them to go
home. Xie suggested maybe no cursing. She told him to
fuck off. Leni rubbed Jo's shoulder. Jo told her to fuck
off, too. Only one person, a teenage girl with a lisp, had
stopped to talk. What are you guys protesting? Leni tried
to answer but Jo cut in, saying, Those clothes in there,
they're made from animals killed in factories, do you get
it? Not to mention sweatshop labor in third world coun-
tries where kids work twelve hours a day in shitty condi-
tions for a dollar a day to make your sneakers. The girl
looked down at her shoes. Leni said, Here, take a flyer.
Trying to smile. The signs bled in the rain. Little river of
dye into the gutter. They tossed everything in a dumpster behind the Gap. I thought it would feel good, you
know, to do something, Xie says. Like, I thought it would
feel like it mattered. But it didn't. Karen shakes her head.
That sounds kind of depressing, she says. Yeah. It was.
They eat for a while in silence. Karen finishes her sandwich, rubbing peanut butter from her thumb onto the
thigh of her jeans. Would you do it again? she asks. He

squints. Go to a protest? No, she says, gesturing, what you did. On the farm. Xie tugs a piece of loose skin from his lip. The ants work a piece of the seed loose, carry it away. He nods. Yeah, why? You don't think I should have? Karen shrugs. I'm not saying that, I just think it made a lot of trouble for you. Xie taking a sip of air. Face hot. At least they got to run. For a little while. Silence. Karen's eyes on the side of his face. He pours some crumbs into the dirt beside the step. The ants make new lines. Quiet. He sniffs. Thanks for the sandwich, he says. Karen swallows. You're welcome.

On the way home he goes again to the broken tree, its leaves browning; detached from its crown the birch has no way to digest the light, leaving the trunk to starve. He strokes its sides. A beautiful thing, still. He lies beside the tree, head on the root, and sleeps.

When he gets home there are two backpacks in the hall, full of camping gear. I thought we could take a trip this weekend, Erik says, folding laundry at the kitchen table. To the lake. Don't you have work? Erik shrugs. I took the weekend off. For what? Just for a change. Unless you have other plans. No, Xie says, That's fine. Thinking of the birch, reluctant to leave the woods, he doesn't need to go somewhere else but maybe that's the point, Erik uneasy about all the time he spends in the same place, alone. And the lake is beautiful and he is asking you, so.

You'll go. Watching the gas gauge on the hour drive, how much burned up so you can get away from the place you came to in order to get away from somewhere else. Nice weather, his father says on the hike in. How's school been for the girls? Good. No one bothering them? Xie shakes his head. When the police asked Xie if he'd acted alone he said yes; but Erik knew, without saying it aloud, that the girls had been there. Part of him upset, maybe, that they have escaped what Xie has not, punishment in all its forms, but it was Xie who had stopped, who had let Moore find him. They're quiet the rest of the way. Shifting their packs. Dull crunch of leaves, heavy blue sky. A pebble in Xie's sneaker, bruising the arch of his foot. Here okay? Erik asks. Xie looks around the clearing, small scatter of trash from the previous campers, blackened ring of stone for the fire. Xie pathologically clumsy with the tent, dropping his end or twisting it the wrong way around, stumbling over the stakes. Erik rattling the nylon. Xie, will you pay attention. Fire slow to start. Evening birds in the trees. His father carving up a piece of wood with a folding knife, thumbing off the rotten bits. What are you making. Star. Is it hard? Shrug. A little. Shavings in a tiny pile between his knees. I'll show you how if you want. Xie snorts. I can't even hold a wrench for two seconds without getting a blister. Erik's small acknowledging smile. You could learn. Can you get us some more kindling? Xie drags a pile of branches to the pit. Don't burn too many of them, it's not that cold, he says, wiping his hands on his pants, and Erik nods, glancing up from the star. I know. Xie walks to the lake. Sore foot shoved into the weed-choked shallow. Afraid of spiders. Lie back. Nest of weeds nudging his hair. Thick gash of stars striping the sky. Lake water numbing his toes. He can smell the branches burning. Stirring the water with his foot. Voices creeping up through the weeds. Men, five or six. Boots just a few feet away, they've almost gone past when. Someone calls. You okay there, little man? Had a few too many? Xie says nothing. They move on. But back at the camp those same men, sitting around the fire, plaid jackets and big arms, his father holding the half-finished star. One of the men turning, So this one's yours? Erik nods. That's my son. Cheers, little man. Drinking from a fresh can of beer. Xie wonders what his father looks like to them, sharp cheekbones, delicate despite his height, all that lean muscle, voice still crisp with his childhood Danish. I'm going to bed, Xie says, heading for the tent. Groans from the men. Come on, sit awhile, we won't bite. What's your little sign on your shirt mean. It means fuck eating meat, he says, and the men explode into laughter, hooting. Dang, boy. To Erik: You got a live one there. Xie crouching into the tent, on his belly in the sleeping bag, listening. They drink and laugh and Erik laughs, too, quiet, and then they go. His father putting out the fire. Hiss of hot wood. Clatter of cans. A branch breaking in the distance.

He wakes up curled against his father's back, cheek between his shoulder blades. Erik too still to be asleep, muscles tense, Xie's first impulse to pull away but. Don't.

You never touch him, he only touches you, less than he wants. So. Stay there a minute. Holding your breath. Finally Erik turns to face him and Xie rolls onto his back, away. Good morning. Morning. Sleep okay. Yes. You. Yes. Xie's heart pounding. He swallows. Gets off the blanket. Granola out of a bag for breakfast, water in the ancient enamel mugs, feet pushed up against the stones of the dead fire. Heard something last night, Erik says. What do you think it was? Don't know. Deer, probably. Xie smiles. You thought it was a bear. Erik shrugs, also smiling. Maybe. Be careful, he says, Xie off to forage, saucepan in hand. I will. Just beginning to recognize chickweed, ramps, oniongrass, but it's the wrong season for those; stupidly excited when he finds blackberries, a few walnuts. He cuts some chanterelles, pinching the leathery stems. It's early still, with that raw feeling he finds only in the woods, chilly, hungover, as if, even after dawn, the trees are still shaking off the night. He digs a hole to piss in, he can't do it like his father, against a rock, into the ferns; he hates to piss at all in the woods, never mind shit. He holds it. No matter what you do you are poison here, disturbing something, hurting something, you're no John Muir or Thoreau or whoever the fuck understands how to live. In this wood alone there are three hundred species at risk of extinction: the black rail, the nuthatches, the gray fox, and you just tromp around pissing like a dumbass. He walks for hours, until the saucepan is full. Wading along the lake, jeans soaked to the shin. Harsh white skin of light on the water. Head back to camp, early afternoon, where Erik is reading, book cracked in half so Xie can't see the cover. Looking up as Xie tucks a handful of mushrooms in his mouth. Are you sure none of that is poisonous? Xie shrugs. Pretty sure. Erik sets the book down, kneels to start a fire, lining Xie's wet sneakers and socks on a rock to dry. Easing beside Xie, hands flat on his thighs, rubbing his jaw against his arm. How's it going with Karen? Fine. She's nice? Xie nods. You don't get bored at home? No. Erik fills a pot with water, sets it over a tiny gas stove. You can still graduate with your class, you know. If you get through these next few months. I know. They eat spaghetti, crackers, tomato sauce. The walnuts are bitter, they spit them into the fire. His father sings a song in Danish. Xie lying on the ground. His father was in a choir growing up and can still achieve a chillingly high note, a boy's note, so out of place in that long body. What are the words about? Erik smiles. Loving your country. Xie sings part of it with him, hiding his voice inside his father's. Later Erik swims, a blond dot way out in the water, impervious to the cold, while Xie walks the perimeter of the lake. They build another fire, eat beans. When Erik goes to the tent Xie stays, stroking the dirt with his shoe. The stars look like chips of bone. Blue. Yellow. He lies on his belly. Rubs his hips against the ground, mouth open. A low breeze caressing his back, his ass, he lifts his hoodie to feel it, fingering his spine. The taste of stone, blood loud in his ears, dirt in his lashes, yes, it's here, the body, beneath you, all the bones you could want. The earth held together by the dead. Grimacing as he moves, feverish, low moan on the wind.

Hips jerking once, twice, then still. In the morning Erik finds him curled near the firepit, cheek pressed against a twig. Clothes cold. Xie, why didn't you come inside? Slow focus on his father, thick swallow, gritty teeth. Jesus. Rubbing his face against his sleeve. What time is it. Six-thirty. Erik's firm grip, Up you go. Shaky legs. Eat breakfast, take down the tent, hike to the car. Red dots where the mosquitoes bit. Come dry on your thigh. The sun flat in your face, burning.

He doesn't tell his father where he goes with the girls on Friday nights and Erik doesn't ask, assuming, maybe, that they are going to their usual haunts: the vegan diner, the university bookstore, Jo's house, as if they have nothing better to do than just hang out, as if what happened over the summer was an anomaly and not the start of a trend or lifestyle or whatever it was that going to the meetings meant they were doing; Xie doesn't know what it means, doesn't ask the girls, just gets into the car. They arrive early, help Peter set up the folding chairs and the card table full of snacks, barbeque jackfruit jerky and compostable bowls of gluten-free chips, Jo pumping Peter for information about the history of the group, its other members, which he provides without hesitation; he knows where everyone was born, where they went to school, what jobs they've had, what other organizations they've been a part of, when and if and for what they were arrested. Shit, you're the feds! Jo says, pointing mock-accusingly at him. Peter laughs, hands up. Guilty as charged. When the others come filtering in he stays with Xie while Jo holds court on a battered couch, Leni perched next to her, giddy, shy, bony shoulders hunched beneath her thin coat. Peter pours himself a cup of hard cider, offers one to Xie, who takes it, hand shaking, it's so stupid, why don't you ever just. Calm down. Jo says you guys did some work with PETA, right? Peter asks. Xie shrugs. Just protest stuff, nothing official. No, that's good, I mean obviously PETA is basically a corporation at this point but that's where a lot of people start, almost everyone here went the same route. PETA, Greenpeace, all that crap. You don't think it's good? Peter holds his hand up. No, no, it's all good. Some people don't mind being told what petition to sign, where to shop, who to vote for, but I really struggle with the essentially conservative position of mainstream activism. It's too slow, it's too rigid, it's too indirect, right? If you're really thinking about food production, about what you're eating, eventually you have to look at land, you look at climate, you start thinking beyond species and you realize that change has to be less about amending the existing system and more about—the big stuff. Peter smiles. Sorry, preaching to the choir. Xie glances at the stairs. Is Nova going to be here? Peter blinks. Nova left last week, I don't know when she'll be back. She's full-time in Central America now, with Earth Alliance. I wanted to ask, actually—did she say anything to you? In the hall? Xie shifts. Um. No, she didn't. Oh. I thought I heard her voice up there. What happened to her face? Xie asks. Peter looks over the rim of his cider. You didn't hear? She was filming an illegal clear-cutting operation in Guatemala and she got caught. Unfortunately, some of those guys carry machetes. Peter swallows, gesturing with his cup. I just don't get why she did it that way. Heck, she has a whole camp of people doing work for E.A., any one of them would have gone with her. But she didn't tell anyone and she didn't look after herself. It's like she wanted something bad to happen. Maybe she thought it would be easier on her own, Xie says, maybe she was just trying— Nothing's easier on your own, Peter interrupts, sharp. That's the first thing you learn. People with that mindset—they're either in prison or they're burned out or they're dead. I knew a girl, a couple years ago, who made a pact with a group obsessed with extinction, every member tying their life to an endangered species, not just mammals but insects, plants, fish, whatever. Her thing was a moss that only grew in the montane forests in Bolivia, where she was born. Everything, her whole life, was about that list. She isolated completely. If a conservation group wasn't focused on exactly that thing, she wouldn't deal with them. In her mind, this was it. This was how she was going to make her point. And when the forest was gone so was the moss and so was my friend. Peter rubs his brow, sweaty, the heat on in the basement, too hot for the weather. I support Nova a thousand percent, but I don't think getting hurt or hurting yourself or someone else does the right kind of good. The work we do can be scary, it can be hard, but it doesn't have to be lonely and it doesn't have to be about despair. Peter drains the cider from his cup. I mean, damn. What a waste, you know? Quiet. It just makes me mad. How long have you been doing this? Xie asks. Twenty years. Lines all around his pale blue eyes. Xie looks at his own cup, still full. I'm sorry about your friend. Peter pats his back. Hey. Thanks. And thanks for being here. Me? Yeah, you. Xie flushes. Um. I haven't done anything. Oh, but you have, Peter says. You will.

It's late when Jo pulls up to his house, the road pitch-black aside from the headlights. Whose truck is that? Leni asks, craning to look at the SUV in the driveway. Xie frowns. I don't know. Ruh-roh, Jo says, eyebrows high, your dad have a hot date over? A hot date with a gun rack? Xie stares at the SUV, knee jumping. We can go in with you, Leni offers. No one, aside from FKK, has ever been in his house. No, it's fine. See you guys tomorrow. He gets out of the car, walks up the path. In the living room Erik on the couch, a stranger beside him. Baseball cap, flannel shirt. Filthy jeans. Hey, Erik says. You're home. Yeah. Nearly a dozen bottles open on the table. This is Jason. From work. Jason lifts his hand; Xie echoes the gesture. He goes into the kitchen. Two bowls in the sink. That your soup I just ate? Jason calls. Pretty damn good. Thanks, Xie replies. He takes a slice of bread from the box, folds it over a banana, walks back through the living room. Jason leaning for the remote on the table, You mind if I change the channel? Erik waving his hand, eyes half-mast. Xie has not seen his father drunk in a long time. Go right ahead. On the screen: some woods.

A man and a boy in yellow jackets. The man saying, Steady now. Smooth shift of gun from side to shoulder, the boy turning his head to sight the shape staring straight at the camera. It's so quick. Shit, Erik says. Jason whistles. That's a beauty. Xie out the back door, screen slamming, over the garden fence, cold slosh through the stream. Feet thrashing through the leaves. Windless. Go all the way to the east end of the woods, where the stream weaves beneath the bridge. The road amputating the breast of the woods, a thick bar of trash lining the concrete where it meets the dirt. Stopping near to scream. Scream and scream and scream. The mink and the library and Mac-Adams and his mother on the phone and Jo's big house and the men in the strip mall and the scar on Nova's face and the vanished moss and the blister on his palm and the way the body folded. The head hitting a stone. The sound of the head hitting. The boy lowering the gun to look. So serious. Pale face. Tentative smile. The legs going out. The eyes rolling back. The stranger inside his house. His own father letting him in. Not knowing better. The buck's head hitting the dirt. You got 'im. Mist of blood in the air. You did good, son. You did so good.

Zigzag through the woods. Throat sore. He knows it's stupid. A deer getting shot on TV, an idiot on the couch, who cares. You do. His mother used to say it was just depression. From her blood to his. Something as simple as sadness, easier to understand than grief. For what. Not for himself. If it was only that, he would just. Die. How much easier it would be. If it started with you, you could stop it. Stop yourself. But it's much bigger than you. Xie looks at the house from the trees, a light on in the kitchen. Night soft on your face. Your back against a tree. The sound of a car starting on your road. Jason gone but you don't move. The shot is still inside the house. It is almost everywhere you go. A thick rain falls, clouds knit hard together. No light from the moon but that old light, behind you, you've seen it every night for a year. You've watched it. It has watched you. The birch it touches luminous and if it is touching you then you, too, must be luminous. It raises the hair on your arms. And the thought hits you as the light hits you as the rain hits you. Get up. Walk the other way. Not to the bridge or to the house or to the road leading into town but the other direction, the only way you have not yet gone. The ground softening with every step, bark peeling in sheets from the trunks. Roots gathering the water, the wood always feeding itself, with the sky and the air and from every death that settles here, holding the land together, holding what is above to what is below; the chaffinch and the primrose, the wood sorrel and the violets, the bluebells and the woodcock. The crows. The pale moths with wings edged in black and brown and white, clinging to the serrated leaves. Witch's brooms of dead twigs spread between the branches. The velvet mosses and ferns pulsing with beetles and worms, army of light and decay, of night and air. The husks of the winged seeds of the trees themselves, rotting since last spring in the seams of the earth. You can see it in pieces or all together, the parts or the whole, a chaotic encyclopedia in every square inch. Xie burrows deeper through the birch. In the city it was bright all the time, everywhere; but here you can track a single light for miles. He slips on a twig, his shoes soaked, hood heavy on his head. Soon he is at the edge, the last line of trees toeing the submerged grass. The light brightest. The light is brightest here.

The church is tiny, taller but no bigger than his own house, planted at the far end of the field. Dark stone and thin windows graze the steep red roof. Silver spire. Peaked wooden door, laced with rusting ironwork. A round window above, and above that the lamp, white light frosting the crumbling steps. Xie puts his hand on the door, pushing: it swings open. Inside there is no one. Two rows of pews, five deep from the altar, an enormous painted cross. A marble font. Stone floor. Enclave with a wooden gate to the right, rows of candles, a handful of them lit before a tall portrait of Mary, head tipped to the baby Jesus against her breast. A piano in the choir loft above the entryway. Stained glass all around: red, blue, white. An angel outlined in lead. To the left, a table with a leather registry, and behind it the confessional, as slim and severe as a coffin. His clothes drip; he turns in a circle of water, looking. He wipes his face with his hands. Holding his breath. Don't think for a sec. He can feel it, whatever it was in the woods. Stands very still. It's here. Right here. Turning back to the door, how did he miss it? A painted cabinet, dark gold, taller than Xie, pressed beneath a sloped stone arch. A little hole, also gold, for a key. Could be coats inside, or whatever priests wear, or Bibles, or. Nothing. Could be nothing. The rain stops. Such a silence, deeper than in the woods, pure, unrelieved. Xie takes a step; he strokes the belly of the cabinet, where the wood swells. He presses his thumb against the keyhole. Bends. Inhales. He knows the smell: cold, earth, bone. The way a smell can be like a sound, calling. The key hangs from a nail behind the case, its long chain swinging slightly against the stone. He slips his hand in the gap, takes the key, fits it into the lock.

How to describe the beloved?

Behind the door a pane of glass, and behind the glass, a body. Full skeleton dressed in an elaborate suit of silver. Knee bent, hip cocked, one hand pointing to the sky, the other settled on the hilt of an enormous sword. Head turned downward in its nest of metal to gaze at Xie. Silver boots to the thigh; long pleated skirt; breastplate in a Roman style. Narrow windows edged in heavy filigree cut over the arms, the shins, the chest, revealing the slim yellowed bones beneath. A plaque affixed to the bottom of the glass: *St. Pancratius. Martyred 304 A.D.* He traces the name. Pancratius. P. So. This is you. Silver cape strapped with more gold to his shoulders, falling in thick folds to his boots, a half dozen chains linked across the breastplate like necklaces, hung with medals. A circle of gold affixed to the back of the helmet, reaching a foot in all directions, as if the skull were a star crowned in fire. Everywhere the metal etched, tooled, stamped in layer upon layer of exquisite designs, not overwhelming the austerity of the bones but highlighting their merciless perfection. Those eyes, pitch-black in the low light. The body liquid in all its hardness, something not fixed but fixing, from boot to crown, the entire room on itself. A warrior. A prince. A king. Flames flicker in the glass. Everything moving and nothing moving. Everything alive and everything still.

He is on his knees at the foot of the cabinet. Face wet. Time sweeps its shadows through the room; wax vanishes into smoke. He thinks nothing; he is aware only of the body, its beauty, its supremacy. How to survive it. A pain, sharp, in his chest. Spreading. Arms eyes thighs head hands heart. Heavy. Full of your own living. The body watching. Knowing you. You stay there. Breathing. As hard as you have ever been. The windows half bright at four in the morning. Eventually someone will come, whoever takes care of this place, of the saint; he has to wipe his prints from the glass, the saliva from his lip. He shuts up the body, slow, eyes on the skull until. Gone. Key in the lock. A sigh behind the wood. The rest of the church jumping into place. Swallow. Slip out the door, down the steps, dew in the grass, sparkling against his shoes. He falls back into the ferns. A whisper in the branches. Help me. A shock of crows bursting from the leaves.

He rides his bike an hour into town, to the library near the university, where he checks out every book he can find with Pancratius's name: *Lives of the Saints, The Golden Legend, Jewels of the Catacombs*. There are dozens of images, not only of the body but of the fourteen-year-old boy to whom the body supposedly once belonged, statues and etchings and icons showing the saint with a lamb at his feet or in his arms, smiling, blond, obedient. Xie in the woods, books open in the dirt, studying each page. How many millions of people have known Pancratius's name, kneeled in his churches. How many believed he had existed and still did. In some way. A soul, a spirit, a body unbound by death. A channel to the sublime. All those believers calling on a boy for help, to cure a headache, a cramp, a disease, to destroy an enemy, to recall a wayward son. To simply. Intercede. Pancratius just one of hundreds of relics dug up from the Roman catacombs and displayed in churches all over Europe, bodies not dressed in armor like P., but draped in velvet and silk and lace, loaded with huge jewels, each bone encased in a fine mesh of gold or silver, the skulls adorned with elaborate wigs, fake eyes, painted lips, how could he not have known? That there was, for a few hundred years, a voracious audience for bodies like this, no shame, no secret, until the fashion for bones expired and almost all the relics were stripped of their treasure and destroyed or sold or hidden away. Lost. The books don't say when P. came to the church in the clearing from his previous home in Switzerland; the last photo of the body was taken there, in an alcove beside the altar of a modest chapel in Wil. Every year, for two hundred years, the body was carried through the streets of his city; thousands got on their knees before him, crying out in joy. A festival. A feast. How many still know this story by heart. A boy on a road in Rome, refusing to lift his sword against a lamb, losing his head every time the story is told, again and again and again.

As soon as his father is in bed Xie is out the door. Lightest wind against his neck. Quick over the mossed log on the stream, through the fence, jump into the soft dirt of the bank and up. Feet snapping through the undergrowth. Full moon. Hands out to feel the trees as he passes, gentle slap against the trunks, fingers slipping over the dark knots in the white wood. Birch eyes. Watching you. Boy in trashed jeans, hood up, a mile in ten minutes. Breathless. Brush of leaves against his face. The light from the church a gem on the slender branches, brighter and brighter, until. There. Deep hush inside. Candles lit, flames straight, white wax piled on the iron shelf beneath the painting of the Virgin, her eyes averted. He takes the key. Open the cabinet. Some sweet scent. All around. Palm to the wood, then to the glass. Warm. Let me look at you. The skull's cool grin. Nest of gold. Look, then. So quiet. The way it grows around you, this space, the air, time itself, as if you are something. Harmless. Belonging. Here. Cheek against the case, both hands, hips. A burning. Delicious. Rocking against the glass, small tide in your body, building, no one can see you, it is you who are seeing, who can see, how beautiful he is, how right you always were, about this, to want it, the shape of the body the shape of desire itself. Then a sigh, not yours; a caress, gliding up your spine:

Beloved.

Not a dream. His voice. From above, from below. Xie jerks back, staring. The face in the case the same, the body the same, not moving but something is moving. Inside and out. The sudden heat, the smell of bone, of earth, the stone, the moon against the windows, and P. like all these things; a fact. Xie turns his back on the body, palms to his eyes, panting. Will it hurt you? The air contracts, gathering everything to a single unbearable point, in your head or outside of it, it doesn't matter. Look at me, beloved. You are not imagining it. It is imagining you. Xie opens his eyes. Whatever you see when you turn will ravish you, destroy you. He turns. As slow as he can. Look. P. waiting. Luminous. Being. Xie shakes so hard his teeth snap down on his tongue, blood at the back of his throat. Whimper bouncing off stone. You could go out, now. Shut up the body, key in the lock, the door closing behind you, why not. Imagine life wandering off in a direction other than the one before you. But you don't imagine. You get on your knees. Head and hands against the glass. Flesh humming beneath that dark gaze. Close your eyes. Hard swallow. I'm here.

You come every night, all night, one week, two, living only at the edges of every moment spent elsewhere; in the library with Karen, at the meetings with FKK, at the table with your father, even in the woods you are waiting to be with the body. Knees black from kneeling. At the glass falling asleep for seconds at a time, sublime exhaustion, the night an infinite cocoon. The voice doesn't come again but you sense it, all around. Waiting as you are waiting. The idea takes shape inside you, wordless; you don't need the voice to tell you what it wants, what it demands. You know how to break a pane of glass. How to hide your face. How much this body weighs: one hundred pounds of metal but only fifteen pounds of bone.

He works in the garden. Tearing out the old dead plants, making plans for raised beds, a cloche system to protect the vegetables in winter; he wants the entire square of earth transformed. He lets his father tell him what to do: weed, haul the dirt, unroll the mesh wire, hammer the nails. Turn the compost. He lays the seeds for broccoli, cauliflower, spinach, chard. Knowing that when they grow he will have to destroy them, in part or in whole, the dilemma of taking life something becoming vegan didn't solve, that nothing can solve; in the scheme of existence, where does the plant fit? The mink? The trees? Xie? The body? Why does one thing have to take a place above the other, any others? He doesn't know. Trying to feed himself, his father, in the least ugly way; it seems possible, at this moment, that he can figure out how. A slim string of calm from the bones to you, from you to this. Make something. So that when he comes it is beautiful. You've been going out at night, Erik says, dragging a bag of dirt to the fence. Not a question. Yeah. Where to? Just. Shrug. Woods. Doing what? Xie sinks a seed into the earth. Um. Walking. Walking? Yeah, just. Around. Is it safe? Erik asks. Why wouldn't it be? I don't know, something might be out there. Xie shakes his head. There's nothing out there. Well, could you stay in tonight? I've got a job in town and I'll be gone until dinner tomorrow. Xie nods, casual, despite the shiver that runs through him. Sure. They raise the last bed onto its trestle, Xie driving the final nail into the pine. Squinting in the dusk. His father's hand on his back.

After dinner Xie cleans the attic. On his knees polishing the floor, laying new sheets on the mattress, clearing out old boxes from the closet. Dish of bones at the head of the bed, a branch on the pillow. The garden is ready; the attic is ready. When you hear Erik's truck disappear down the road you drop silently down the stairs, black mask, black pants, the hammer in your hand.

At the threshold of the church you pause. Face slick beneath the mask. Wait for the fear to kick in but it doesn't come: no one can hear you, stop you. Robed in the fresh dust of the woods, lungs drunk on its air. Pushing the door open. At last. You recognize the quality of the silence that always fills the church, not absence but expectation, a bubble longing to burst. The cabinet, freshly polished, as smooth as satin in the candlelight. The key gleams on its chain. The doors fall open and the body looks down at you, ravenous. Hand tight on the hammer you tap the glass, one, twice, then again, harder, full swing, and it falls like water, shattering over the stone. Splinters of glass cling to the black mask, in the fibers of which your blood remains, from the last time; you can still taste it. Shaking free of the shards. Hands trembling in the gloves. Climb into the case. Dust and bone and silver. Bracing your back against the wood. Deep breath. Leaning to put your mouth against his teeth, eyes shut tight as you let the kiss run through you. Beloved. Hand against his cheek. His brittle face. What you have waited for. Then: get the body free, strips of old leather strapping the body to a post. The knife cuts through the skin with a snap. In an instant he falls into you, groan of metal and velvet and bone. The glass cracks beneath your shoes. The body sighs. The crown slips from the skull. You put it on your own head.

The only way to get the body through the woods is to drag it, walking backward, skull pressed facedown into his chest. Boots digging into the underbrush. Ferns shuddering in their wake. Starlight striping the length of the cape, shadows gathered in its stiff folds. Lone owl. Rustle of fox. He has to go slow, step carefully, arms and legs burning. Weave through the birch. Past the dead tree. The stream peeling back from the rocks. Walk right into the water. Splash and drag. Pull him through the gate. The sunflowers nodding on their stalks. Panting. Stepping over the threshold and something like gold, coming from the body, all around. No time to marvel. Still the ladder to go. Will have to. Undress him first. The wide skirt, the breastplate, each long boot, hinges at the back stiff with age; he takes it all off, exposing the armor's lining of thick red velvet, unfaded, wet from where the water came through the boots. A pile of silver and gold on the living room rug but the treasure is here. Can you believe. That it is yours. The body pure, unadorned, so small without its armor. You must. Take care. Skull against his chest, legs hooked over Xie's arm. Up the steps, then laid gently on the bed, quick stroke of the ribs and then several trips for the armor, stacked in the back of the small closet, the cape the hardest because it is almost too wide to fit, it scrapes the paint off the wall as he wedges it through. Lock the door. There. Turn to see. The skull nested on the pillow, barely a dent. Look at me. He kneels on the mattress, naked. Candlelight brightening the sides of the bones. The ribs a narrow bell, holding their fistful of air. Xie's hand where the heart would be. He caresses the spine, the most beautiful, reptilian line in the body, fused with glue to replace the lost tissue; the coccyx, hands, feet, and jaw also glued, too delicate to articulate with the crude metal joints fastening the rest of the bones together. Only the bones held in place by the meat of a living body have been lost; the patella above the knees, three tiny bones in the inner ear. Otherwise the body is complete. He crouches between the femurs, kissing the top arch of the pelvis as he fits his arm through the gap, slow, as far as it will go, all the way to the shoulder, filling the hole with his flesh. Hand crawling up the spine, vertebra by vertebra. As deep inside the body as it is possible to be. He lays his head on the thigh, his arm gleaming between the wings of the pelvis, twisting beneath the ribs, finger grazing the darkest place on the body: the foramen magnum, a jagged circle the size of a silver dollar floating at the bottom of the skull, through which the spinal cord once connected the rest of the body to the brain. He fits his finger inside, stroking the dark interior of the skull, stirring its most private air. Certain that no one has ever thought to touch the body. In this way. For pleasure, to give pleasure. Hands trembling. Heavy breath. Do you like this. Cradled between its legs. Stroking the body from the inside. And then there is P., kneeling on the mattress, behind Xie, spirit but solid, a body as tangible as the bones, dressed as he was in the case, radiating that gold light, which is yet another body: the saint split in three. It's the spirit that speaks, that says the word again: Beloved. The light over the sheets, crawling up Xie's thighs. Xie turns the body over on its side. Belly to spine. Kiss at the top of the neck, hand skipping over the back of the ribs, gripping the crest of the hip. Holding your breath. The light stretching all the way to your neck. Turn me to gold, too. Let me drink it. Touching the body all over. P. touching you. The body draped now over yours. You have the skull in your hands and the light is. So bright. Pinning you to itself. Lips against his forehead. Against his mouth. Not hurting anyone. No. No one. Kissing the breastbone, the clavicle, the cheek. Dry, impossibly light. Perfect. The candle lit. A deep shadow over the body's face, skull tipped forward, mouth against the bottom of the jaw, Am I all right, do I look all right to you. Beautiful. Yes. Show me. How hard you are. Let me hold you. Come, P. says, beside you, caress from temple to hip. The body above you. A bird's weight. Rapture. Beloved. Thrusting up. Deep shadow. Deep night. You are. So. Happy.

Waking to the body against his, rib to rib, foot over foot. Long look at the skull, slow kiss. Not a dream. Before getting out of bed Xie takes the sheet and wraps the body. Careful as he straightens the legs, smooths his hand over the pelvis. Someone walking into the room would see only a pile of blankets on an unmade bed; you'd have to know the body was there to see it. Sun settling on the pillows. Dust rising from the mattress, fractions of skin and bone. Smell of sex. While he showers P. leans at the sink, watching through the curtain. You don't have to be with the body? Xie wonders. P.'s grin. I am anywhere. Beckoning. Let me see you. Xie turns off the water, dries himself. P's head dipped to his neck. Don't make me hard again. Light against his back. Xie arching into it. Fingers against his throat. Even in the mirror you see him. The glass, the room, you: full. Gasping into the sink. Finish dressing, no breakfast, hair still damp as he pulls his hood up. Come with me. Through the woods. The birds calm in the trees when P. passes. Faint tracks from the night before, the drag of the body's boots in the dirt, half covered with fresh leaves, the marks of other beasts. The birch not yet bare, leaves just starting to turn, branches a fragile lattice against the sky. Squirrels circling the trunks, reminding Xie of the mink, wary eyes, soft bodies. Where are the bones of those creatures, he wonders. Scattered over the roads where they were crushed, buried in the backyard where they were found biting the necks of someone's chickens, silver chins matted with blood. All of them shot. He saw the pictures in court, someone giggling behind their hand as Xie wept in his, Ryan Moore gazing at him with the mild wonder of one animal about to eat another. Moore will pack his yard with mink, install a security system, a steel gate in the driveway. With Erik's money. But don't. Think about that now. P.'s boots ringing on the library steps. Ducking to keep his crown from hitting the jamb. Inside, Xie half expects P. to disappear, but instead he grows larger, illuminating the hideous room, grazing its low ceilings, the dusty stacks. Radiance. Pouring through the plate glass, splashing the cement walls, a man asleep at a table meant for a child, sweat glittering on his filthy brow. Hey, Karen says, folding her jacket over a chair. You're bright and early. He nods, sitting. Yeah, I. Stops. Trying not to stare at P., sitting beside them. She blinks. You okay? Yeah, I'm fine. Hand over his mouth, trying to wipe the grin off, can't. Sorry, I just. Didn't sleep much. The sharp lip of P.'s boot cutting into Xie's knee, can he really feel it or is it. Just his imagination. Another nudge: Can you feel that, beloved? Stifling a laugh. Opening his textbook to the chapter about the Spanish Inquisition. Xie giggles, helpless, forehead to the page. Seriously, Xie. Do you need to go outside for a minute or what? Deep breath, palms against his eyes. Straightening his face. No, I'm sorry. The fire alarm goes off. They both jerk in their seats. Jesus, Karen breathes. Someone sheepishly shutting the fire exit door. P. by the fire alarm box, one finger beneath the plastic cover.

At home his father back, television on. Xie glances at the attic door, desire so intense he can taste it: sulfurous, like licking the head of a match. Everything go okay here? Erik says. Yeah, fine, Xie breathes, perching nervously beside his father, doesn't he feel it? P. glowing behind the couch, the body over their heads. Erik points to the screen with the remote. You hear about this? Xie blinks. A nun clutching a rosary, broken glass at the bottom of the case, P.'s sword on the stone floor, the church itself banal on-screen, lusterless in the afternoon sun. The news anchors speculating about black markets for Catholic treasure, Satanists, meth addicts. It is an unspeakable offense, the nun says, the relic is priceless, it is a body of God. A photograph of P., shown from crown to chest. The newscaster describing him as a *macabre seventeenth century antique*. Can you believe that? Erik says. Practically next door. Weird, Xie whispers. The weather comes on. Gold dripping from the ceiling. Which is it. Hallucination. Macabre antique. Body of God. Beloved.

———

As it gets colder, the meetings get longer, fuller, no beer but plenty of hot tea, which Xie drinks nonstop. Having to pee every fifteen minutes. He knows a few of the other people by name, exchanges small talk, reads the notices in the bulletins, but Xie always ends up with Peter, whose eyes find his as soon as they walk in the door. Hands on Xie's shoulders, little slap from behind. Listen, there's a group of us thinking about occupying the rodent research lab at the university, I thought maybe you'd like to join us? Next weekend. Xie flushing. I'm still on probation, he says, if anything happens, like, the littlest thing—Peter groans. Hey, I didn't think of that, sorry. Next time. Friendly grin, as always, no big deal, but Xie can't meet his eyes. If something happens to Xie then the body is alone. Unwilling to risk it for some mice in a lab, admit it, you came here with FKK to do what Peter's asking you to do and now you just want to be home. With it. Pathetic. Xie rubs his face on his sleeve. He goes to the bathroom again, then slips out the door, you never touch it without thinking of Nova bursting through it, why can't you tell anyone. About what she said. That furious smile. He walks the perimeter of the building, his breath white in the air. Hands half frozen inside his hoodie. Such an enormous church, twenty times the size of the one in the woods, merely functional: ugly gray stone, no candles, no colored glass. P. never comes here, is never anywhere with regularity except the woods, the attic; he is not a dog, he won't come when you call. Xie passes a window, ankle-height, opening onto the basement. Peter's red head bent toward Jo, Leni on the couch with her arms around her knees, watching a video on someone's phone. As far as he knows, most of the saints worked alone. When they brought Pancratius to Diocletian he was already an orphan. After he refused to kill the lamb he was beheaded with the same knife he had been offered, but first he was forced to watch the flesh of that other neck part from bone. A god bleeding at the feet of its deniers before becoming, once again, merely an animal. Through the window Peter takes the box of produce you brought from your garden and passes it around. Leni takes a tomato, the first you have grown in the cloche, and feeds it to Jo. You can't think, now, about those mice; if only you could explain why. What would it be like. To say his name out loud. To publicize the most private ecstasy. But then it would be destroyed; Pancratius knew this, that to speak of the beloved was to invite death. He did it anyway. How can anyone know you, if they don't know this. Does it matter. If in truth you are barely here. He goes back inside. I'm sorry I can't come to the protest. Peter waving his hand. No worries, farmer. Next time. Tiny broken veins in Peter's cheeks, his nose, loose stomach stacked above his belt. People age out of radical activism, he had said once. They move on. But not Peter. Xie looks around the room; there is no way to know who is here to learn how to make vegan mac and cheese and who is here to build a bomb. Jo in the car saying, Don't worry, we'll represent. You know the researchers get the mice pregnant just so they can cut the babies out of them while the mothers are still alive? Leni in the back with Xie, her boots in his lap, no seat belt, cheek cradled against her palm. Jo, could you just not talk about that right now? Why not? It's what they do. They put them on these tiny crosses, I mean they literally call them *cruciform*, and they pin their legs— And Leni half shouting, as mad as she ever gets: We *know!* We just spent two hours watching it on the stupid video! That look in her eyes the same as in those of so many of the people in the meetings, a mixture of hurt and fury, everyone sick with what they read, see, feel. Knowing you could break into a lab and fuck with shit all you wanted but there would always be more people who thought it was okay to drive a knife into the belly of an animal than there were those who knew it was wrong. Did it hurt, he asks P., in bed, touching the neck of the body, between the fourth and fifth vertebrae. Did it hurt knowing you would die or was it a relief. P. doesn't answer, lying beside the bones, the light settled all over, gold on silver on gold. Impenetrable. Supreme. Xie takes the jaw of the body between his teeth, gentle: you will never get over this taste, part earth, part air, P.'s hand on your cheek, bridging flesh to bone with a spirit belonging to neither, free, and for a moment you can believe, surrounded by the beloved, that death has never visited any body for long.

So I have the stuff in here, Jo says, the boxes in the popped trunk full of empty canisters, filters, spare fuel lines. Unfolding a thick packet of paper covered in diagrams and smudged green ink. Erik frowns, squinting in the dim light of the garage. Whose instructions are those? A guy in town wrote it out for me. He done this type of conversion before? Jo shrugs. His friend did one. Erik looks at her, then pulls his phone out of his pocket. Reads. Xie helps Jo unload the equipment onto the table in the corner, plus four gallons of used vegetable oil that smell like rancid french fries. Erik props up the hood of the Jetta. You sure you want to do this? he says. It's a nice car and it may not run the same. Yeah, she says, I'm sure. What about your parents? Jo grins. I'll say you had nothing to do with it. We just need to like put in the new fuel system, settle the oil for a week, and, boom, we'll be ready to go. Great, Erik says under his breath. Barest hint of rain in the air, more of a mist, sun filtered gray onto the blacktop through the garage door. Jo rests her knee on the fender. Can you show me what's up? she asks, and Erik makes room, head leaning close to hers, low voice, See this? Xie goes inside to make lunch. P. at the stove, stirring a pot of chili. Xie takes a tomato, a knife. Spill of seeds. P.'s perpetual grin. Is it soft, beloved. Yes. Pressing a piece between his teeth. P. drawing in the juice on the cutting board, the tip of his finger turning red. *Fidelitas.* What does it mean, Xie asks. It means that you are mine. Jo bangs in and he freezes. Almost sure no one can see but still. It scares him. Though she is just pouring water. Thinking he is all alone. Xie wipes the knife over the juice on the board, clearing what was written there, folding the tomatoes into the pot. Jo's hands black to the wrist, grease on the glass as she drinks. Your dad is being fucking awesome about this, by the way. Squints. What's on your lip? Um. Xie wipes his mouth. Just tomato. Jo bends over the stove. When did you learn how to cook? He shrugs. About the same time I learned how to garden. She hits his arm. On our commune, you're the housewife, 'kay? 'Kay. She goes back through the door. Xie takes a bite of the chili. Burns his mouth but swallows. Another bite. Another burn. He laughs with his mouth full. What the hell is the point. If you burn french fry oil you're still putting nitrogen in the air, you are still. Driving your filthy fucking car. Leaning over the sink, the laughter drying up. He snaps an arm from the aloe plant on the sill, rubs it against his lip. Why did you laugh like that like you are losing your mind. P.'s hand on his chest. Sliding up his neck, his chin, his forehead. Seeds in the sink. Finger bones tapping his temple. Stand up, beloved. He stands. Breathes. His father's footsteps at the back door. Xie? You okay? I'm okay I just. Burned my mouth. The beans spitting down the sides of the pot. Erik cuts the flame. Angles to look at Xie's face, pulling away the aloe. Squints. You're fine. Don't eat out of the pot. Xie snorts. Yeah, right. The mist clinging to the window. Thanks for doing this, Xie says. Erik nods, scrubbing beneath his nails with a brush. I'm happy to. I just hope it works okay for you guys. Jo revving the engine in the garage, her ecstatic whoop. Xie presses the arm of the aloe back into the dirt, lip throbbing. Above the sink three heads reflected in the window, P.'s crown gleaming between Xie and his father. Erik catches his eye in the glass; he smiles. Xie smiles back.

———

He sits at the base of the thickest birch. Owls. Mock-ingbirds. Rustle of mice. Shine of centipedes. From here he can see the light of the church. Not afraid of it any-more. Loves it. Loves that it is always there. Sometimes he goes to light a candle, sit in the pews. Someone built this place knowing hardly anyone would come; there is so little room for those who do. And yet. Here it is. The grass high at its sides. In the missals: *I look forward to the resurrection of the dead.* And back through the woods with P.'s hand in his, to the dark house, to the body, fresh from the night, the window open, the sound of the stream. The body in his arms. Candles stuck all over the floor, he stole them one by one from a local craft store. Matchbooks free from the tobacco shop because the owner likes his patch that says *Take Nothing, Leave Everything,* he laughs and says, But you take my matches. Borrow pinecones, pieces of bark, stones, black feathers from the woods to dress the body in, the dish of bones at the head of the bed. Rub the skull with oil. Tie a piece of grass around the finger for a ring. You wear the crown. Wish you had the sword, but the real one is in the church and P. never lets you touch his. Pretending to make cuts with it all over your body. Once held it to the back of your neck. Could he do it, if he wanted. Kill you. He can make his body so heavy against yours, can appear twice as large as he was in the church, impossibly tall, his armor un-tarnished, his sword ablaze. In the woods, he bends you over a stone, lifting his skirt, you pant into the moss. You fuck the body but P. fucks you. How is it different from what so many others experienced, Maria Galluzi, Matilde of Magdeburg, Teresa de Ávila filling page after page with lust for Christ, a desire so consuming it could fill a mind, a room, a life. But you want the vessel, not just the light; you want a hand, a face, a shape, and that is what you have been given, though you can't understand why, when you don't even believe in gods or spirits or saints. Why, when you have faith only in this one life, did he show himself to you? You don't ask. You just close your eyes and let him come.

At Jo's, pumpkins lit up on the lawn, a huge cauldron belching smoke. Jo dressed in a brown curly wig and overalls patched with blood, Leni with a monocle and Victorian skirts shredded at the hems, a stick of dynamite strapped to her boot. What are you? he asks. Guess. He squints. Both of them have red smeared over their mouths, black beneath their eyes. Zombies? Zombie *feminists*, Jo says. I'm Andrea Dworkin, obviously, and this here's Emma Goldman. And what are you? An eating disorder? Xie shrugs. Just bones. Jo shakes her head. That is incredibly basic. They sit on the porch handing candy to trick-or-treaters and watching Jo's parents' friends drink red punch ladled from a crystal bowl filled with plastic eyeballs. Hey you, a woman says, tight black dress, knee-high boots. Too cozy next to Jo. Beautiful night, isn't it? These your friends? Leni smiles, skittish. Introduces herself. And who's that there? the woman says, leaning to look at Xie, who ducks his head. Jo smirks. Oh, that? That's your worst nightmare, she says, teeth stained pink from the punch. Xie chuffs. The woman laughs, short, dismissive. Well, you guys look great. We're not guys, Jo says, and the woman blinks. What? You called us guys, there's at least two women sitting here. Oh— I'm sorry, young *ladies*, the woman says, smiling, and Jo smiling back, but mean: You really need to think harder about the gender bias you're enforcing in your everyday speech. What? Jo lifts her chin. You heard me. The woman's smile collapses. Well, I will certainly take that into consideration. A pause. Xie looks at his hands, white tendons painted over black gloves. Flex. Unflex. The woman pushes herself up from the step. Nice to see you, Jo. They watch her go. God, who was that, Leni asks. My dad's boss, Jo says, lighting a cigarette. His *boss*? Leni's mouth open. Oh my god. Xie shakes his head, You say "guys" all the time. And Jo's grin, Yeah, but I'm not a clueless twat, so. Shrug, dragging on the cigarette. They sit until the candy bowl is empty, then heave up from the porch, striking through the crowd, out beyond the circle of yellow light toward the woods. Xie pinches Jo's cigarette from her fingers. Don't. Folding the warm butt into his pocket. A year ago she would have rolled her eyes but now she nods, Sorry, sorry. No flashlights. Strong moon. Is it full? Leni squinting. Nah. Almost, though. No birch here but thousands of ash, sweetgum, deep red leaves gone black in the dark. Impossible not to step on the seedlings, there are so many, and no paths; his hand on Leni's shoulder, stepping where she steps. We should sleep out here, Jo says. Leni grimaces. I don't want to get eaten. No one is going to eat you, Jo scoffs. Except Jo, Xie says, a moment too late but they still crack up, hushed, the light of the party dwindling behind them. Blue line of mountains flat against the sky straight ahead. You can pretend that this is all there is but you know there is a golf course a mile to the east, bigger than this patch of woods, and Jo's father owns part of it. Xie has never asked what it's like for her, to have the same last name as the one on the billboards, her father's big grin looming over the freeway. A kiss of wind against Xie's face. Kicking up the dust of the dead leaves. You know Nova used to come here all the time, she writes about this exact place in her book, Jo says. How she came out here after her dad literally disowned her. A branch whips against Leni's head, knocking her monocle from her eye. He *disowned* her? That's fucked up, she says, fumbling for the monocle in a patch of ferns. Where is she now? Xie asks. Is she coming back? Jo grins, mock-spooky voice: Nobody knows. Seriously? Yeah, seriously. After the meeting she kind of disappeared. She's probably in Guatemala kicking some corporation's ass and the fewer people who know about it the better. Xie thinks of the way Nova looked before she left the church, both freer and more trapped than anything he had ever seen. They stop at a clearing, a few charred trunks marking the bald spot made by an old fire. Sit in a circle. Eat hard candy from Leni's pockets. It's so crazy about that skeleton that got stolen, Leni says, stroking the sleeve of Xie's costume. I've lived here my whole life and I didn't even know that thing was there. Did you? Xie rolls a stone beneath his shoe. No. Nobody did. Yeah, except the guy who stole it, Jo says. Do you think it was Satanists like they said? Leni asks. If there were any Satanists around here we'd definitely know who they were, Jo says. It was probably some weirdo who actually goes to church. They're the ones who put him there in the first place. Like how can you call Satanists weirdos if you're the one going around digging up bodies and dressing them up in crazy shit? Leni tips her head back, dried blood stuck in black gems all down her throat. I think it looked kind of cool. If I was a skeleton I'd want to look like that. But they locked it away, right? Yeah, because they knew it was fucked up. Jo cracking a lollipop between her teeth. Xie rubs his arms. These woods not like his, thicker, darker, more fragrant, denser canopy means denser decay, so much rot all around. Half of the woods in the county cleared in the last thirty years, and in his lifetime almost all the rest will join what has vanished. Life cut down and down. Leni taps Xie's shoulder with her stick of dynamite. You always smell so good. Quality vegan diet, he says, and she shakes her pink hair. Nah, she says, grinning. It's the sweet scent of celibacy. Jo cackles. Xie's flinch hidden in the sockets of his makeup. From far off the sound of a coyote. Do you hear that? They do. Going still. Jo howls, head back, and Leni and Xie join her, first for fun, then for real, louder and louder, until Jo's phone rings. She answers. What, she says, then rolls her eyes, hanging up. It's my dad. He says they can hear us all the way at the house. She lifts her middle finger above her head. Can you hear this? she shouts. Leni snickers, pushing on her arm. Jo puts her head in Leni's lap, reaches to touch first Leni's pointy chin, then Xie's white cheek. I love you and you. Closing her eyes. The coyotes sing. They sing back.

P. glows so strong in the morning, at the window, making signs on the glass. Check the body to make sure. Nothing hurt or broken. How long can it last, this way, outside the cloistered air of the cabinet? A lifetime, at least. Wrap the sheet around the body. Dress. He makes bread, then cooks the oats that have been left to soak overnight, ready for his father, who eats them with an entire package of fake bacon. Can you die if you eat too much soy? Erik had asked once, faux-casual; Xie just shrugged. Probably. Goes out to the garden. The broccoli ready to harvest, the cauliflower, big creamy heads cradled in green. He runs his hands over them, lifting the leaves, checking for decay, mold, insects, disease, the same as he checks the body every morning. Moore probably does the same, every day, walking his rows of mink, making sure nothing will spoil those silver furs. Another kind of farmer. Deer surround the house. Flicker of ears in the fog. He struggles with the stupid hose. Glitter of dew in the webs clinging to the eaves. The morning sun on P.'s teeth. In the attic he wraps the body in a blanket, pulls the sheets from the bed, and carries them to the garden to shake free all the dust from the body, settling finer than ash on the pumpkins. When the sheets are clean he hangs them in the cold sun. The only sound the pins creaking and the wind ruffling the crowns of the trees and the water smoothing the stones. Xie's sleeves pushed to the elbow. P. stroking the tender flesh at the inside of his forearms. How soft you are here. How like silk. The sheets pressing against Xie's legs. Immense stillness. The sun so strong and the air so clean and the smell of the sheets and earth and turning leaves. Xie closing his eyes. There are eight beds now and two cloches for the carrots, parsley, radishes; all of it his doing. Rows of jars in the pantry; counters covered with chickpea seedlings. P. chewing a stalk of grass. Thumbing the wrinkled leaves of the mint. Everything feels something, knows something. The heads of the nasturtiums nodding in the breeze. Every stalk and leaf stirred. Soaking up. And P. in the mint, Are you not also a child of God?

He hasn't been to the city since they moved two years ago, but for Thanksgiving a plane ticket arrives in the mail, his mother on the phone: You're not even going to school anymore, what is so important out there that you can't come see your mother for a few days? Because there's a body here, he wants to say; because I can't leave it. When he tries to refuse his father takes the phone, says, Of course he'll come, he can't wait. He exchanges the ticket for one for the train, adding two days to the trip but there is no way he will get on a fucking plane and he wants to tell her so, but Erik shakes his head. Just take the shuttle to the airport so she can pick you up. Why? Erik digging his palms into his eyes. You know why. The watchword of their life in the city being, Don't upset your mother. So. Long goodbye to the body. P. off in the corner, liquid, not touching the sheet. The body resting on one hip, the knees nested together, the feet like bunches of twigs, brown and yellow, tangled at the base of the blanket. Skull turned into the pillow, tight jagged lines meeting where the three plates of bone fused solid, back when the body was a baby and the skeleton still soft, swimming inside its sea of flesh. He takes the hands in his. How light its touch is, mothlike, a creature devoid of violence. What if. Something happens. Nothing will happen, beloved, P. assures him. But when he shuts the front door he feels the sudden absence of them both. Turning to look over his shoulder. Where are you. The attic window dark. He takes his keys from his bag, hand against the door, but Erik calls, We'll be late. Xie hesitates on the step, stomach cold, wiping his mouth on his sleeve. Drops the keys back into the bag. Alone on the train, just. Sleep through it. Neck bent. Hood over your head. The hours melt over the windows, light to dark, dark to light, a man asking you to move your bag off his seat, thigh touching yours. Shrink up. Almost there. Finally at the station, then shuttle to the airport and Ellen with her enormous sunglasses and gold sandals reaching for him. Reek of jasmine and shampoo. Oh, my baby, she says, kissing his head. You have your bag? This is it, he says, indicating his backpack. Honey, that's all you brought? Yeah. Travel light, I like that, Jerry says, clapping his shoulder with a grin, loose cotton shirt and long shorts, younger and shorter than Ellen, who leans against his side as if unable to stand without him propping her up. Backseat of their pristine SUV freshly vacuumed, air conditioner blasting. Ellen pats her hair. Gosh, you're skinny, honey, you know that? Your dad says you do all the cooking. I don't remember you being into that, are you sure you can manage it? How are your studies with that tutor? I saw her photo online, she's very cute, his mother says. Very cute. Xie scowls. What does that have to do with anything. Ellen glancing at him in the mirror. It might actually be for the best, you know, this tutor, a more structured environment might speak to your learning style. She huddles around a compact, plucks a stray lash from her eyelid. The edge of her dark hair, almost as dark as his own, ironed flat as a sheet of paper. She slides her sunglasses back on. Do you have friends you want to see? He puts his head against the seat. No. Usual traffic. The car barely moving. You should have let me take the bus, he says. She snorts. Buses get caught in traffic, too, you know. Endless ribbon of asphalt cut into the dry hills. Treeless. What would P. make of this landscape. Does he even know it exists. Are you hungry? Jerry asks. No. Eating a handful of almonds. Once at the apartment heading to the bathroom with his bag, crouched on the tile to unfold a square of flannel. Splinter of bone no bigger than a needle. Jagged on one side from where it fell away from the marrow. Five minutes, ten minutes, Xie wedged between sink and tub, the bone beneath his thumbs; this is where you used to come to look at that photo, of the skeleton at the head of the tomb, you left it beneath a stack of towels in the cupboard once and when you looked for it again it was gone. Ellen at the door. Xie? Do you need something for your stomach? Not answering. Erik in the house, not knowing. The body above his head. Please let it be okay. You kiss the bone. Fold it up, tuck it away. Water on your face. Everything in the apartment fresh, faultless: white tile, gleaming mirrors. But so small. No room anywhere and outside no yard, no land, you can hear every move anyone makes in this place. Jerry whispering to his mother, Just give him some space, he'll warm up. Drink from the tap taste of fluoride and lead spit it out. Whisper. Come get me. Curl on the floor. Close your eyes. Wake up.

I'm going out for a minute. Ellen at the table, eating macaroni salad. Where? To the beach. Jerry nodding. Good call. The weather is freaking unbelievable. I read they're finding dolphin corpses on the beach, Xie says. Ellen scrapes up more macaroni. Jerry scoffs. That's some sonar thing. Xie shaking his head. There's no Navy testing in this area. Jerry's brows go up. Hm? Navy testing, Xie repeats. They're the ones that use the sonar that affects marine mammals. Jerry's indulgent smile. I'm pretty sure it was something to do with sound that caused those dolphins to get mixed up. Xie shrugging, hand on the door. Pretty sure it's more likely that the half-million tons of oil spilled into the ocean four years ago have something to do with it but. Whatever. Slipping out. Careful not to let the door make a sound as it closes. Such sun. Tree-less. And the pavement. Blinding. Ellen lives just three blocks from the beach; he and Erik lived several miles inland, on the east side, but he came here every weekend. All the garbage in the water, bodies in the water. Fisher-men gathered on the cliffs, tossing white sea bass and mackerel into buckets. On the pier once he kicked one of those buckets over, the fish pouring, green and silver, back into the sea. The fisherman, barely older than Xie, yelling, What the fuck! as he chased him, hands almost on his back but Xie jumped in front of the cars passing through the toll arm, the fisherman shouting for some-one to grab him but no one did. He avoided the pier after that, even though a part of him thought he should do it again, do it every day, get arrested, get hit, who cares; a year after the spill the fishermen back out there, willing to eat or sell whatever they could find in that dead water. Xie steps off the boardwalk into the sand. Usual jam of people, bright blue water. He climbs over the long flat piles of shale. Not a single starfish or anemone or crab in the tide pools; instead thin lines of orange on the rocks, and on the sand three dense fists of tar. He makes a shal-low bowl with the hem of his hoodie and scoops them up. Sound of volleyballs thrashing against nets. Laugh-ter. Watching the tar balls tremble as he walks home. The oil harmless if left in the ground but poison up here, if you put something where it doesn't belong it dies or it kills or both. Not its fault. He doesn't look again at the water, dazzling behind him. At the apartment he dumps the tar directly on the kitchen counter. What's that?

Jerry says, chopping garlic. It's tar from your perfectly recovered beach. It's what? It's oil, Xie says. Washing his hands with half of a lemon. His mother looking over her shoulder from the stove. Xie, what's wrong with you, get that off the counter. We're eating in an hour. I'm not eating. His mother protesting, shoulders up, The turkey is free-range. It's organic. I made sure. Mom. I stopped eating meat three *years* ago. She flaps her hand. Well, eat the potatoes, then, I don't care, eat the green beans. Jerry slides the tar into the trash, the balls trembling against the bag of turkey guts. How is Erik? she says, leaning forward to try the gravy, lips peeled back from her teeth. He's fine. Jerry, she says, and Jerry turns, sleeves rolled, rubbing his hands. What can I do? The turkey, she says, and he actually replies, Oh, boy. Xie puts the potatoes and green beans on the table, opens the can of cranberry sauce, slides it onto the plate. You need to cut that. I know. Cutting it. Beautiful color. Congealed blood. The table only seats two comfortably. Barely room for the stuffing, the gravy boat, the rolls. Cut glass dish full of butter. Xie touches his silverware. Think of it like. A dream. The two of them sitting there. Smiling at each other. Jerry leaning to rub her thigh. Thank you for this, honey. Jerry folding a piece of skin into his mouth. Xie dips the roll in a smear of cranberry sauce. Gets through a couple bites, spits the last into his napkin. Don't you want some vegetables, Xie? Jerry asks. I don't eat animal products, Xie says, and Jerry, confused, staring at the green beans, How is this— Butter, Xie interrupts. Butter is from milk, which is from cows, which are animals. Jerry blinks. Gosh, I didn't even think of that. Sorry. His mother's fork hitting the plate every time she stabs up a forkful of food. There is music on, something classical, cheerful. What are you thankful for. The yellow walls and white woodwork. Gleaming steel appliances. The vintage china plates with real gold on the rims. Silver candlesticks. He goes to wash the dishes while they finish. Come watch a movie, she calls, and they do, Xie on the floor, his head against the leg of the couch. In the middle of *Home Alone 2* his mother touches his hair. It's so soft, she says. Jojoba oil, he says. Mm. She falls asleep and Jerry carries her to bed. Their door shut. Xie stares at the television. Turns it off. He opens a window and instead of the sound of the stream the sound of traffic, the browning fronds of the palms dotting the boardwalk, endless stream of lights through the glass. Distant scent of ash from a fire somewhere in the hills. His mother laughs in the other room, about to get fucked by Jerry. Nowhere to go. Xie punches his thigh, once, twice. Doesn't feel it. Knuckles pressed between his teeth, bone seeking bone, You fucking bastard, are you real? Then show yourself.

He wakes up. No clothes. He left them folded on his backpack. He goes to the laundry. Yanks the clothes from the dryer. His mother drinking coffee at the counter. I thought that could use a wash, she says. He holds his hoodie against his chest, breathing through his mouth to avoid the hideous smell of Tide and lavender dryer sheets. Yeah. Thanks. Dresses in the bathroom. Blue bruise on the side of his thigh. He makes sure everything is in his bag. Flannel and splinter of bone. Safe. Xie, his mother says. Her thin smile, slick with gloss. I thought we could go shopping. Shopping? For clothes. What, he says, no, I don't need any clothes. My treat, she says, and he sighs. Only if we go to the flea market. But there's an out-let mall, she says. I don't want anything new. But that's what you need. You can get stuff that looks new at a lot of places, he says. And it's cheap. Fine. Okay. But *no* holes and *no* rips or stains or anything that smells. He rolls his eyes, tosses a pillow at her. She shrinks from the pillow as if from a punch. Xie, *don't.* Scowling. As if she can't tell that he's just playing. Sorry, he mumbles. They walk to the market, jammed with people, stalls, dogs, bikes, the crowds fattened by the holiday. His mother puts on her sunglasses, dipping her head, thin hands shaking. It's very busy, she says. Mom, it's fine, he says. Both of them breathless. Sweating. What to do in a crush. If you are being crushed. He herds her onto a side street, marginally quieter. Takes a breath. Oh, this is cute, she says, fingering a flannel shirt. Isn't this what you wear? In the country? He blinks. Um. And it's warm, she adds. You can wear it over your T-shirts. No, I just. I wear this. Tenting his fists through the pocket of his hoodie. Well, what do you wear on the days you don't wear that? No, I wear it every day, he says. Well, it certainly *looks* that way, Xie. Girls don't like a ragamuffin, she says, look-ing through the racks. He digs through a box of jeans, finds a pair he likes. Gray. No holes. His size. Goes to the seller, a young man with hair to his shoulders sitting in a lawn chair, legs crossed, headphones on. Hey, Xie says. Reaching into his bag. I'll give you some jam for that pair of jeans. The guy guffawing, What'd you say, man? Xie shrugging. It's good. I made it myself. And the guy reaching a skinny arm toward the jars, examining them. Blackberry, no shit, he says. His mother coming down the aisle with a shirt in her hand. Xie, what are you doing? Just bartering. *Bartering?* As if he'd said, *Selling heroin.* The guy grins. Okay, dude. Deal. Taking the jars. Xie slinging the jeans over his shoulder. His mother openmouthed. The guy scooping out a finger of jam. Hey, man, this is incredible. Leaning forward for a high five. Turning toward Ellen. You got anything for me, lady? And his mother putting her wallet back into her purse, saying firmly, No, as if teaching them both a lesson.

Jerry drives because his mother can't get out of bed. She took Xie's hand, little rub of his knuckles with her thumb. 'Bye, honey. Be good. 'Bye, Mom. In the car a medal of Saint Christopher hanging over the mirror. Xie squints. Are you Catholic? Jerry's eyebrows, What? The medal. Oh. Oh, yeah, no, that was just—my sister gave that to me, kind of a joke, because of the way I drive. It's for protection or something. That's Saint Frances, Xie says. What? Saint Frances is the patron saint of drivers. Not Christopher. Oh, is that right? But I thought Francis was the animal guy? Xie's brow furrows, No, Frances with an *e*, she was— Xie shakes his head. Never mind. Quiet as they pull onto the freeway. Endless road. Tom Petty on the radio. Hey, Xie, Jerry begins, voice falsely bright. I wanted to have a little talk with you. Xie scrubbing his forehead with his palms, thinking Shut up shut up shut up. You know, we've noticed, your mom's noticed, how you seem—like it's hard for you to enjoy things? Do you think that's fair? I mean, I really respect that you're interested in certain diets and protecting animals and stuff but it seems like those sentiments are being expressed in a, in an unhealthy sort of way. How so? Well, like getting in trouble out there. I didn't get in trouble, Xie says, sharp, thinking: I'm not the one in trouble, you are, they are, everything is. I think your parents would disagree, right? I know your mom has been really concerned about everything that's happened. I mean, we just want you to think about how your actions might affect your future. College, that sort of thing, right? Xie nodding. No prophet is acknowledged in his own village. Saint Christopher swinging against the mirror as they stop suddenly. Xie's knee banging into the dash. Jerry yelps. Sorry! Guy cut right in front of me, jeez. Gripping the wheel. Two yellow rubber *Live Strong* bracelets on his wrist. Could you drop me off at the train station, Xie says. What's that? Could you, he enunciates. Drop me at the train station. What for? Xie's head back against the seat, eyes closed, almost dead. Taking his last breath to say, Because I'm taking the train, you fucking idiot.

As soon as he is off the train he is blinded. Gold from horizon to sky. Stumble into it. Erik's hand on his shoulder.

You okay? Xie smiles. Yeah, fine. The city far behind him.
Into the car, P. in the backseat. Black sockets in the mirror. Roll down the window. Fresh air. Chin on the glass.
How was it, Erik asks. Xie sighs. She washed my clothes.
With Tide. Shit, Erik laughs. Xie laughs, too. They eat
bean burgers, play cards. After dinner Xie says, I'm really
tired. Tries not to rush up the attic steps. Climbs into
bed, pulling the blanket over his head. Hand around the
back of the skull, cradling it to his neck, as close as he
can get, leg between leg, chest to chest. The smell of him.
Dust and. Clean. Where were you. P.'s hand between his
legs. Xie holds his breath. Doesn't matter. Here now.
Long caress. Black under the blanket. Slipping his fist
beneath the ribs, the heart right here. Scooting down to
lick the hips. Arm oiled from wrist to shoulder, to ease
it again through the pelvis but this time from behind,
pillow beneath the ribs, the oil everywhere, spine wet,
scapulae, two fingers sliding through the foramen in
the skull, steady, delicious. I'm inside you. Yes, beloved.
Still stroking. It goes. On and on. P. behind him. Hand
to spine. Knee to knee. Are you close. Fuck, don't stop.
Don't stop. The pressure of P.'s presence, almost unbearable. Why are you like this. So strong. I can't. Stand it.
Xie on his back. P.'s head between his legs. Don't think.
What it would look like. To anyone else. His face between your thighs. Hands beside your cock. Mine. Yes.
Yours. Whimper. Fingers deep in the sheet. Turning to
lift your leg over the body, come darkening the bone.
How careful you have to be, with a body like this, or it
will be destroyed. You can never forget, for even a second,

what it is, what it needs. Do they all deserve it, every creature of the earth, to be touched like this, fucked, loved,
adored, a stone, a sea, a fox, a tree. Can you see everything
as a body that is crushed if not cared for, a body capable of
ravishing and waiting to be ravished, gently, completely,
by life itself.

I have your grades, Karen says, pushing at a yellow envelope. Congratulations. You're barely passing. Folding her
arms. Something intimate about her anger, as if she has
the right to care this much, what does it matter to her if
he passes or not, she gets paid either way. He sniffs. Hands
in his hoodie. She lifts her chin. Well? The clock ticks.
He doesn't want to touch the envelope, to look at her. He
should just. Go. Knee jumping. Who does she think she
is. Who he is. She stares, nostrils flaring. Finally he leans
forward to slide the printout from the envelope. Scanning
the slim column of Ds, a single C, in algebra, surprise surprise. Chewing his lip. He rubs his nose. It's not you, I just.
She looks at him. Oh, I know it's not *me*. Xie backed into
silence. Wary. I mean, either we're doing this or, I don't
know, she says, chin wrinkled. Stripping a hangnail from
her finger. I'm sorry, he says. No, Xie, you're not sorry. I
don't need you to be sorry. Sitting back, hard, chair leg
skipping against the carpet. Look, it's the last day before
break, so let's just get your reading list in order and set up
the date with the counselors—Xie startled, I have to talk
to them—? Of course you have to. Why? You have to meet
with them every semester, Xie, Jesus, have you not been

paying *any* attention? Gesturing with the envelope. Xie rubs his hair with both hands, head down. She takes a breath. I looked at the packets you've been turning in and it's different work, Xie, you're not giving them what we're actually doing in here. That's—you have to explain that to me. Xie shifts his feet beneath the table. I just don't want them to have it. Have what? Anything. Anything real. From me. Of mine. She looks at him. What do you mean, real? He looks back. Doesn't answer. Then why not quit? Your dad? He shrugs. Yeah, I guess. She doesn't say, You're so stupid, you're doing twice the work to screw no one but yourself, she just lets what he's said hang there, her eyes still dark. Well. I guess you can do what you want. We could just sit here and do nothing. Voice shrill at the edges. He blinks, head back. What? she says. You don't want to do the work, don't do the work. Gnawing viciously on a thumbnail. Karen, he says, and she shakes her head. I'm pregnant. Immediately raising her palms as if to ward off the effect of her words. I shouldn't have said that. I'm sorry. Silence. She opens a textbook at random, pushes it toward him. He pretends to read it as she sits, chewing the same nail. He writes something meaningless in his notebook, turns a page. An hour limps by. She checks her watch. Do you want to get something to eat? Xie asks. Karen shakes her head, shoving her things into her bag, careless. Take the rest of the afternoon off, she says. The zipper of her jacket cracking against the table as she stands. Enjoy your break. He tries to catch her eye but she looks past him, keys in her hand, on her way out when Greg stops her, asking her for something, a book past due. I don't have it, she says, and when he tries to insist she repeats, louder, almost yelling, I don't have it! Her bag banging against her hip as she walks out the door.

Midnight Mass. A pocketful of mushrooms. P. stripping a piece of bark from a tree; Xie eats it along with the mushrooms, old medicine, flavor of soil and wood, that hint of poison in each; too much and you will be sick, just enough and you will be healed. A wreath nailed to the church door, pine needles sprinkled over the steps. Light in all its colors coming through the glass. He stands near the cabinet, back against the stone, pushing the hood from his head. A woman in a red coat turning to look; she smiles. Xie smiles back. The priest in a white gown. The room fuller than he has ever seen it; ten, maybe a dozen people. Smell of incense. Sound of singing. Christmas carols. How does he know all the words, he wonders, when he can't even remember ever singing them before. But maybe he did. In school or. Somewhere. P.'s cabinet open, the case full of poinsettia plants, plush red leaves stroking the sword. The parishioners line up to eat the body, to drink the blood. If you really believed that was what you were doing, how did you explain it to yourself, how did it feel. Like excitement or dread or. Something else. Passion. Putting their lips to the cup. The woman in the coat crossing herself in front of the cabinet, head bowed; P. behind her, touching his hand to her head, her gray hair stirring. The parishioners raise their arms for the last prayer. Xie slips out, P. following. As soon as the church is behind them Xie takes P.'s hand, greedy, jealous, pressing it to the back of his own head: I am the only one you may touch, no one else. P. pulling him close, mouth against Xie's forehead. Do you miss it? Miss what, beloved. Being there. P.'s cape stroking the grass as they step into the woods. I was never there, beloved. A nuthatch swooping through his shoulder. His face the color of the trees, fresh milk poured against the night. The nuthatch, along with two-thirds of all bird species in the town, in the state, in the country, will have vanished by the end of the century: to look at the face of the bird, folding its wings on a branch, is to look at the past. A ghost. A corpse. Do you know what a mass extinction event is? Yes, P. says. A rapture. Let me show you. Drawing a line along the base of Xie's head, that spot where the skull meets the spine, both bones so vital, so vulnerable, split in a second, a great flash of light, white as pain, as pure, the spasm of every nerve's journey interrupted, and then a fountain of blood, gushing up to splash the sword, burning, a rejection of everything; a bone is an atheist, and the sword is Christ, taking his last breath.

At the doctor's office. No reason, his father said, just a checkup. Careful not to say: You've been acting weird lately. Staying out late. Sleeping in. Dark circles under his eyes. Always distracted. New lock on the attic door. So. Twenty minutes to town. Long wait in the lobby. Some fish in a tank, weaving through a hunk of neon plastic. Thin bright bodies. Violet light. There is a woman asleep on a bench, her head tipped against the wall, her purse on her lap. Mouth open. Lipstick on her teeth. You crush up the bodies of bugs to get a red that deep, carmine, he can't remember if it's the actual blood of insects or something else. Smashed-up carapace. Brains. Guts. Erik sighs, legs twitching. What are you reading? Xie tilts his book to show the cover, on which a woman in a white gown looks up in astonishment at the shining figure of Christ: *Interior Castle.* Is it good? Erik asks. Xie shrugs. It's okay. Who's it by? Um. A Spanish nun. A mystic. Erik squints in surprise. A nun? Xie nods. What does it mean? The title? It's about. Um. Praying. And how when you get really good at it, it's like you move through these differ-ent rooms, which she calls mansions, but the mansion is God or something, or the way to God, and the better you pray the deeper you get inside it. And then what? And then . . . you get into the seventh mansion and you. Um. I don't know. Die or marry Jesus, or. Go to heaven. Huh. Are you into praying now? Xie's knee jumps, little laugh. Um, no. It's. Just. For school. They're teaching Catholi-cism in your school? No, I—it's history. English. Histor-ical English texts. I thought it was written in Spanish. Xie sighs. I mean, it's just a book. For reading. Erik shrugs. Okay. Glad you're enjoying it. Xie looks back at the page. *He thinks that people to whom God grants these fa-vours must be angels; and, as this is impossible while they are in the body, he attributes the whole thing to melancholy, or the devil.* Teresa doesn't say how you know it's not melancholy, those favors, only says that when you feel God you know it's him, though elsewhere she says there are people who think they know the difference but are mistaken, so how could you know which one you were, right or wrong? He folds the corner of the page. Nurse calling his name. He follows her into a beige room that smells like Band-Aids. Asked to undress; cold in his underwear, shifting his ass on the paper-covered table. A panel on the ceiling painted blue. For a few months in the city he had a therapist who had a painted panel on her ceiling, too, a woman who was always smiling, even when she asked him if he ever thought about harming himself, if he ever felt like he wanted to die. He never answered. The doctor comes in, a middle-aged man with a gray beard, looking at a chart. Hello. Squinting. How do you pronounce your name? Xie clears his throat. Zee. Like the letter. The doctor sniffs. Huh. Interesting. Setting the clipboard on a desk. So. Just a checkup today? Fingers on Xie's neck. Fleshy thumbs. Xie tries not to move his head away. Light in his eyes, his ears, his throat. Hands against his chest, his back. The blood work you did earlier showed some mild deficiencies, the doctor says. You're vegetarian? Vegan. So no dairy, eggs, fish? No animal products, Xie says. Well. That's fine, as long as you watch your iron. Do you take a multivitamin? No. Scribbling something on the clipboard. You should. You're underweight. Any issues with fatigue? Sleep? Xie shakes his head. No.

Convinced there is some sign on him. A smell. A scar.
Does he smell like bones to other people. Do other people even know what bones smell like. I see in your history you've taken Paxil. You still on that? Little inhale.
No. Are you experiencing any symptoms of depression?
Anxiety? Xie brushes his hair from his eyes. Thin paper
rustling beneath him. You sexually active? He blushes.
No. Well, stay safe if you decide to be. Gesturing with his
pen to a basket of condoms on a shelf next to a coverless
children's book. Making some note on his clipboard.
You're all set, the doctor says. Take those vitamins. Out
in the hall the woman is there, rubbing her front teeth
with her pinkie. Smiles at him. She'll be next, on her
back, this man's fingers inside her. He doesn't know
how women can stand it. How anyone stands someone
getting inside. He has to turn sideways to get past her.
His father waiting in the reception room, reading *Interior Castle*. You don't know what he thinks, when he isn't
thinking about you. You never ask. You don't know if he
prays, and if he does, to whom; you don't know what he
believes, what he hopes, what he wants. In every room
of every mansion Teresa describes the soul struggling
alone; to get to the seventh mansion it must leave everyone and everything behind. But she never says why. Dad,
Xie says. Erik looks up, folding the book in his hands.
Hey. All done? Everything good? Xie's mouth jerks into
a smile. Everything's great.

———

At the store, shopping for New Year's dinner. The girl at the checkout someone from MacAdams. Eying him up and down as she moves his things across the scanner. Hey, she says. He nods, quick glance then away. Money crumpled in his fist. She squints at a package of wheat gluten. What even is this stuff? Xie shrugs. It's um. Wheat for making seitan. What? It's, um. Gluten. Just. Protein. She looks at him. Huh. Handing him his change. Haven't seen you around lately. Yeah, I'm. Working with a tutor for a while. Off-campus. Oh. Well. Happy New Year. Outside it's beautiful. Pure cold. Blackest sky and snow, in huge flakes, swirling in the lot. Ahead of him Karen hurries to her car, fingers hooked through plastic sacks full of groceries. Hey, he says, fingers brushing her arm, tentative. Hey, she says, turning to smile at him, genuine, radiant; so this is how she looks, he thinks, when she is happy. He takes her bags, cold hand brushing against hers. You with your dad? No. She gestures with her keys. Get in and I'll drive you. I'm okay. You don't even have a coat. I don't mind. Well, at least come and warm up with me a minute. Opening the door for him. He tries to find a place to put his sneakers down among the trash on the floor; water bottles, napkins, gum packets, an empty pharmacy bag. Sorry, she says, leaning to pluck a brown banana from the dash. She rolls down her window, tosses the banana into a hedge, rolls the window back up. She runs the heat, rubbing her hands together in front of the vents. So. I've been thinking about you. He makes a face. No, I have, she says. Nothing bad. Laughing. You always expect the worst. I do? I mean, you always have this look like someone is going to give you bad news. He scratches the side of his face. Are you gonna give me bad news? Little smile. Hands in his hoodie. The opposite, I hope, she says. Look, next semester we can just forget all the MacAdams stuff. Read what you want, study what you want, talk about whatever you want to talk about. It really doesn't make a difference to me whether or not you learn algebra. I don't want to get you in trouble, he says. Don't worry about it. As long as you understand the consequences, it's fine with me. Better than fine. It's not like I enjoy all the stuff, anyway. A pause. She ducks her head toward his, trying to catch his eye. What do you think? Yes? No? I, he starts. Confused by how different she seems, all that anger vanished. Maybe she decided. To be happy. So he should be happy, too. He nods. Okay. Thank you. She puts her hand on his wrist. You're welcome.

In January Peter throws a party in honor of Alias, co-founder of Earth Alliance, fresh from an anti-fracking action in Romania. Late Saturday night and barely thirty degrees outside, snow flurries evaporating in the halo of a bonfire lit in a field far out of town. The crowd clustered on canvas chairs and vegetable crates, Peter manning a table of kegs and pots of lethally hot vegan chili. Alias sits on the dirt near the fire, an arm wrapped around long legs, wary deep-set green eyes in a face so perfectly boned Xie imagines, for a moment, what it would look like stripped of its tanned skin. Xie and FKK sitting with a knot of girls everyone calls the

Prima Zapatistas because they sell black knit masks in-set with custom designs for exorbitant prices. He tries to drink his chili, sucking chunks of bell pepper from the lip of his cup, as Jo describes the protest at the university lab; someone had tipped off campus security and everyone was rounded up before they even got to the science hall, ordered to stay on the other side of an invisible line between the lab entrance and the street. Same old shit, one of the Zapatistas sneers, Peter's actions are always super-weak. I heard you got a lot of signatures for the petition, though, Xie says, people didn't even know what was going on in the labs and now they do. It's not his fault the cops interfered. The Zapatistas exchanging a glance. Do *you* even know what's going on there? Xie frowns, confused. What? The Zapatistas roll their eyes. Silence. Finally Jo scraping the heel of her boot in the dirt. Relax, people. Heavier snow falling outside the circle of the fire. Alias suddenly loping over; the Zapatistas sit up in unison as he tips his beer in Xie's direction. You Xie? Um. Yeah. Alias nods. Glad to know you. Holding Xie's gaze for a moment, shoulder cocked beneath his open jacket. Peter passing beer to FKK, Leni downing hers in three big gulps, moon-eyed while Jo fiddles with a stud on her bracelet. You get your license renewed? Alias asks, turning to Peter, who burps into his fist with a self-conscious smile. Yeah. Finally. License for what? Jo asks. Hunting, Peter says. Xie's startled shoulders. What, Alias says, you've never heard of hunt disruption? No. You must not be from around here. Leni says, He's from California. Then blushes. Ah. West Coast brother. Where

out in Cali? L.A., Xie says. Alias stretching his legs toward the fire, nodding. Long sip of beer. Well, if you get a
license you can go out wherever the hunters are, fire into
the ground or whatever. Lets all the critters know they
gotta clear out. You have to be careful, though. Sniffs.
Guys find out you're fucking their shot, your ass is toast.
Xie glancing at Peter. You have a gun? I have three, Peter says. Grew up shooting. Jo winces. Jesus. You ever kill
anything? Peter looks into his beer. Sure. Lots of things.
Deer? Peter nods. Deer, rabbits. Foxes. Ducks. Ate it all,
too. Leni shivers. Peter squints at Xie. Any shooting near
your place? No. You know who owns those woods? No.
I've never seen anyone out there. Alias fishes a chunk of
tempeh from his cup of chili, chews. Enjoy that while it
lasts. Catching Xie's eye. Xie looks away. What did it feel
like? Leni asks, quiet. Peter leans into the fire, elbows on
his knees. What did what feel like? Killing something,
she says. He scratches his beard. Brief look at the ground.
Good, sometimes. A pause. Leni tucks her hands into her
coat sleeves; Jo kisses the side of her head. The fire snaps.
Alias tilts the lip of his cup into Peter's. Hey, keep up the
good work, brother. And you, farmer. I have high hopes
for you. Xie wondering what Peter's told him: about the
mink, obviously, everyone here knows about that, but
what else? Nothing else to tell. Xie goes to get more chili,
trying to warm his hands around the hot cup. Someone
pulls out a guitar; the Zapatistas sing, half-ironic, the
lyrics to "Which Side Are You On?" while Peter and Jo
march arm in arm. Finish the food, edge away. Up the
hill, through the fence. Crawling into the backseat of

Jo's car, smell of pine and smoke, faint scent of french fries from the cooking oil Erik siphoned into the gas tank from the bottles in Xie's garage. Brush the snow from his hood, then rest his cheek on his knees, sneakers on the lip of the seat. Wait for P. Try not to think about. Peter with a gun. A knock at the window. Alias leaning heavily against the roof, forearms framing his face. Can I come in? Xie opens the door. Scoots aside. Strong smell of beer. You don't drink? Alias says, when Xie refuses his cup. No. You off yeast or what? No, I just. Don't. Usually. Alias nodding, so tall his hair grazes the roof, flannel shirt tight around his arms, jeans worn white at the knees, white long johns beneath. This is someone who U-locked his neck to a bulldozer. Who helped bomb a chicken processing plant in Texas. What are you doing here? Xie asks. Me? Just hanging out. No, I mean. Xie gestures, Back here, in the States. Alias shrugs. Just seeing friends. Taking some time off. Am I allowed? Eyebrows. Xie flushes. Yeah, of course. Alias's slow sigh as he turns in to Xie, hand against the side of his neck, thumb circling his cheek. Xie ducks, shoulder up, understanding too late that look at the fire. Cold out here for you, chickenbones, Alias sings. Little smile, last of the beer, settling his cup on the floor between his spread knees. How old are you. You wanna fuck shit up or what? Save the whales? You should be back there trying to score some pussy. Or are you off that, too? Leaning to brush Xie's hair from his ear, swift shift onto one knee, pressing Xie against the door, wet mouth catching his. Xie whimpers, arm against Alias's chest. What? Alias says.

Come on. Leaning into him. You got something better waiting for you at home? Hm? Saving up? Reaching to feel Xie's crotch and Xie gags, hard, Alias jerking away, arm up, The fuck is wrong with you? Xie curling against the door, eyes squeezed shut. The snow gathers on the glass. Alias rubbing his lips on the back of his hand. Bitter smile. Not into it, huh. Too bad. The car as cold inside as it is outside, low whistle of wind as Alias opens the door, unfolding into the dark. Good luck saving the planet, farmer, he says. Xie wiping his mouth on the inside of his hoodie. Tremble all over. Waiting for the girls and then they come at last, jogging half frozen to the car. We saw Alias come out this way, Leni says, panting. Did he follow you? He doesn't answer. Jo and Leni exchanging a look. Did he? Xie tucks his chin into the neck of his hoodie. No, he says. They turn onto the road. Jo's eyes in the mirror, her hand on Leni's thigh. At home, in the attic, your arms around the bones, you know you will never be in another bed, with another body. Living or dead. The smell of smoke in your clothes. Like something burned up for good.

Monday morning a little late but Karen not there yet. He waits at their table, eyes on the parking lot. Ten minutes pass. Fifteen. Twenty. Tapping his pencil over his notebook. P. in her seat. Boots crossed in Xie's face. Can almost see. Up his skirt. Where is she. P.'s shrug. How should I know. Greg beckons him from the front desk. Holds the phone. Xie jumping up to take it. Karen saying,

Sorry, I'm going to be late. Could you go over your essay for Mead's class and fix all the comma stuff so I don't have to do it? Her voice on some sort of edge. He agrees. Back to the table. P. now in Xie's seat. Xie sits on top of him. Taking a guess at the commas. Erase some, add others. P.'s hands on his hips. Will you. Stop. Karen will be here any minute and. The clock says almost noon. If something is wrong with Karen then it's like a punishment, for not taking this seriously. P. catching this thought, Now you are thinking like a Christian. Shut up. Scrubbing his eyes. Why don't I know where the fucking commas go. Come, P. says, walking to the bathroom, huge, cape grazing the carpet. Inside the bathroom full light. Fingers at Xie's belt, Xie's back against the filthy wall. Hands on P.'s shoulders, cold metal; remember how it was, when he was behind glass and you could not. Touch him. All this still just a dream. P. drawing him out. Tugging. Xie not breathing. Over in a minute, come sliding down the fold of P.'s skirt, pearl on silver, on gold. Fingers on his neck. There are twenty-seven bones in the human hand and you have kissed every one. P. cleaning himself in the mirror. Xie shivers. Zips up. When Alias does whatever it is he does, with boys or girls or whoever, he must imagine it's like this, that he is like P., capable of giving pleasure just by existing. All those eyes around the fire, admiring him, wanting him. And yet he followed you. How stupid can a person be. P. gone. Dark inside the bathroom without him; they hadn't turned on the light. When he comes out Karen is there, looking at his essay, jacket skewed over her shoulders, as if she put it on in a hurry.

Karen, he says, and she turns. Pale. Hi, she says. Come
outside with me for a minute. Xie follows her to her car,
in the corner of the parking lot, Karen leaning against
the hood. Hands in her coat pockets. He offers her a car-
rot; she refuses. You eat like a horse. Not as much as a
horse, but literally like a horse. Xie shrugs. Yeah, well,
horses are pretty healthy. Both of them quiet for a while.
The muscles in her jaw keep twitching. He gestures with
his elbow to her stomach. Shy. Can't quite say, How is it,
how are you. Karen squints. Hard rub of her toe against
a piece of gravel. Slow shake of her head. She pulls a pack
of cigarettes from her bag, a lighter. He eats his carrots.
Karen stubs her cigarette out before it's half gone, brushing ash from the hood of the car. Offers him the butt;
he takes it to the trash. There would have been bones in
it, he thinks. The clavicle in its place, spine growing its
first spiked knobs. Boy or girl or whatever it was meant
to be. He gives her his apple. She takes it. Do you think
it's wrong, she says, quiet. What? She looks at him, brow
knit. You care so much about life. I don't think you're
wrong, he says, and she catches the distinction, between
it and *you*, and nods, head down. Touching her elbow to
his, sleeve against sleeve. Hands him back the apple. He
finishes it. Core into the hedge. Is it better than putting
it in the trash? she says. Something can eat it, he says.
Squirrel or something. Yes, she says, pinkie pulling at
the corner of her eye. Something. Deep breath. So did
you think about what you wanted to do? Yeah, he says.
I want you to read this. Pulling *Interior Castle* from his
pocket. She takes it without hesitation. Okay. We'll talk

about it. What else. He thinks. I don't know. Maybe we can talk about gardening. She laughs. Gardening. Great. He wonders if it happened before Christmas, or after. If she was alone. She has never mentioned a boyfriend, a husband; he can't remember her mentioning anyone else in her life at all, a friend, parents, siblings, nothing. Back inside, she opens *Interior Castle*, turning to the pages he marked. *But note very carefully, daughters, that the silkworm has of necessity to die; and it is this which will cost you most; for death comes more easily when one can see oneself living a new life, whereas our duty now is to continue living this present life, and yet to die of our own free will.* What does this mean, she asks, gesturing with the book. Xie bites his lip. I think the silkworm is supposed to be the, um, the soul, he says. She blinks. The worm is the soul? The, um, the old soul, I think. The one you have before you meet God. She rubs her face with both hands, pale brows wrinkling beneath her fingers. Are you sure you don't want to just continue with the algebra? Xie opens his mouth. She nudges his knee beneath the table. Just kidding. She keeps reading. He opens his own book, *The Golden Legend*; Saint Lucy has just torn out her eyes, in the same year when Pancratius lost his head. *Light is beautiful to look upon; for it is the nature of light that all grace is in its appearance. Light radiates without being soiled; no matter how unclean may be the places where its beams penetrate, it is still clean.* What about the places it doesn't penetrate, he thinks; inside a body, a mind. Glancing up to watch her read. You would be a really good mother, he says, quietly, and she holds her breath for a moment, wiping her fingers beneath her eye.

At home he opens the fridge, shakes a box of rice milk, drinks the last thin slosh from the carton, leaving it on the counter for his father; Xie hasn't taken out the garbage in years because if he does he will end up immobilized in the driveway with a pile of his own shit. I think Karen had an abortion, Xie says, watching Erik fold the carton in half with the side of his hand. Erik frowns. What? She told you that? Xie shrugs. Sort of, yeah. Why would she talk to you about that? You don't need to hear about her personal life. Xie slicing a head of cabbage, its leaves shattering crisply on either side of the knife. He puts a piece in his mouth, chews, adds the rest to the soup, carrots, parsnips, sweet potato, corn, no recipe, just what is on hand, not thinking, pinching herbs from their pots: parsley, basil, oregano. Chopping, slow, the tiny dark wet edges clinging to the blade, he hates to cut, to pull the vegetables from the beds, he knows all about chemical terror in plants, their sensitivity to danger, to death, nothing ever. Simply submits. He slides the herbs into the bottom of the bowls. Tip of his finger against the blade. He breaks up a sheet of crackers, puts them on a plate. Did Mom want to have an abortion? he asks. Erik pauses. Did she what? Did she want to have me. Speaking into his soup. The herbs floating in a circle. Why do you say that? I'm not judging her, I was just curious. Erik lowers his spoon, looks directly at his son. We both wanted you very much. But you didn't plan it? No, but that doesn't mean anything. It's okay to tell me the truth. I am telling you the truth, Xie, what the hell. Dropping a cracker in his bowl. Didn't you know it would be hard? Why would it be hard? Because Mom. Had problems. Your mother's problems aren't your problems, Xie. I just don't get why you would take the chance, Xie insists. What chance? She was pregnant and she had you and we were happy with that. We didn't think of another option. There was no other option. Okay? Erik snapping more crackers between his hands. He knows his father eats meat outside the house, has seen receipts, fast-food cups and burger wrappers in the truck, they had fought about it before and Erik had said, exasperated, I do it your way all the time, every day, I eat what you want, I buy what you want, why isn't it enough? But it isn't enough. Erik putting his spoon down, a little too hard, dull thump against the tablecloth. Look, if your teacher has an abortion it's because she has reasons for not being a mother, and I can't speak to what those reasons might be, but I can tell you that it's not a choice I would have made because I don't think the world is made worse by bringing a life into it. But what if that life is evil? Xie says, thumbing his water glass. Erik's hard squint. You mean you, or . . . ? I mean life. Shrug. Human life. Xie, I'm losing the thread here. Xie takes a deep breath. Did you talk her out of having an abortion. Erik staring but Xie just sits there, waiting him out, until Erik gives up, face hanging over the awful soup. In the beginning, yes, I did. Silence. Sorry, this is crap, Xie says, reaching for his father's bowl, but Erik says, Leave it. Chewing the uncooked carrots. Xie goes to the kitchen, gets a bar of chocolate from the panty, eats it square by square in some weird penance; he doesn't even like chocolate. Erik puts his hand out; Xie passes him the remainder of the bar. How's the garden doing with the cold? Fine, Xie answers. Looking out the window. Scratching his cheek. Erik leans across the corner of the table. Takes Xie's face in his hands. Kisses it.

Beloved. Wake up. Four in the morning. Still so dark. Reach for the bones but P. says, No. Xie stares. P. not playful, not grim; something in between. What is it. P. turning to the door in the floor. Points of his crown sharp even in the dark. Making their own light. Come, beloved. Dressing in the cold. Down the ladder. Over the fence and across the log and deep into the trees, flesh still asleep. He rubs his eyes, sleeves pulled over his palms. Where are we going. Lightest dusting of snow like glitter in the dark. The ground so hard beneath his feet, cold slicing up his lungs. Fifteen minutes. Silence except for. Sound of P. Then. Look down, P. says. Xie looks. Kneels. Spot of gold against a black carpet of leaves. Digs to pluck it free. Tiny cross on a fine chain. How did it get. Here? P. putting Xie's back against a tree. Laying the necklace around his throat. Tucks it beneath his collar, frozen kiss against his skin. P.'s hand against his cheek, hard, P.'s thumb against his chin, pulling his mouth open so he can graze teeth and cheek and bone against Xie's lips. Unzip of jeans to make him come over the ground the snow melting on the tip. Ragged gasp and slap of P.'s hand against his face to make him shout don't question it. You were afraid when you saw him the first time and you are still afraid. Kneel, P. says. Xie immediately on his knees. Lifting the silver skirt. Tilt of bone to Xie's tongue. Thumbing the wings of the iliums, which flare out from the spine like the split peel of an orange, revealing the great hole of the pelvis, the fruit of the body, of all bodies, which is nothing, which is air. Sneaker against trunk, Xie braced between columns of birch and bone. Licking the tip of the coccyx, angling his head beneath P.'s hips to reach it, the tiny rough knob warm and wet from his breath. Between his own knees he could, if he looked, see the first touch of dawn spreading like frost on the shins of P.'s boots but his eyes are closed, he is half freeze, half fire, cocooned beneath the skirt, knees aching. P.'s sigh and then. Silence. Xie wiping the saliva from his chin, forehead against pelvis, his own crown of bone. Scatter of squirrels through the brush. P. says, Shh. Distant footsteps through the leaves. If someone saw them what would they see. Heart pounding, hand to chest as if to silence it. Two voices. Far but not so far, not far enough. Something hard hitting the trunk of a tree. *They're straight and healthy, good size.* Slowly, P. lifts his skirt, like a curtain, the woods a stage. Slap of cold. Bare branches and the air glittering with ice. Two men. One Erik's age, big belly in a down vest, the other young, not even thirty, old sheepskin coat and dark hair to his shoulders, rolling his boot over a stone. Bright orange eyes of their cigarettes. If they look in Xie's direction they will see him, hunched over on his knees, brutally exposed; P. can't or won't hide you. You stop breathing. Fear and fury pinning you in place. *Should have time to do the first batch end of summer, don't you think.* The young one nods. Sucking on his cigarette, eyes narrow, he's only. Two dozen trees away. Private property. If they find out you are here they can stop you. From ever coming back. The young one takes a step, puts both hands against a tree, tips his head back to look at the crown. *Beauties*, he says, and you squeeze your eyes shut, shaking all over. When you open them again the men are turning, backs to you. Moving off until. Gone. Branches shivering above them. Why did you let them in here. P. silent, cocking his head and for a split second you see P. as others might: a monster, along with the trees, the men, you, there is no difference, an immense and grotesque disorder at the heart of all things. Xie gags into the dirt, still on his knees. The utter stillness of the birch, of P., watching. Did you know they were coming. Silence. Did you bring me here so I would know, too. Silence. Then the sound of P. kneeling, chest against your back, hand over your eyes. Jaw against your ear. Silence.

He walks back through the woods, arms burrowed beneath his hoodie, legs stiff. Snot frozen in his nose. Breath hanging in the air. Fuck, he chants, fuck, fuck, fuck. How did you not think. That this would happen. When you know that nothing is safe, ever, did you imagine that he would keep this for you, the way it is, as long as you wanted it, that the birch would be protected because you love them, because of P., because you are a fucking goddamn idiot. And now you have how many months? Before they come back? When you should have known, as soon as you saw the trees, as soon as you moved here, how to protect them, should have started the first night, it is your responsibility, but you thought you thought you thought. You were safe. Here. You slither through the fence, slip on the log covered in ice. P. drags you across by the wrist. You have to help me. Hush, beloved. Opening the back door. His father stirring a pot of oats for breakfast, turning to watch Xie slam into the kitchen, breathless. Hey, where were you? Xie brushing past. Xie, Erik calls after him; but he doesn't answer, impatient, can't explain, unlock the attic door, shut it behind you. Scrubbing your cheeks with the cuffs of your hoodie, What's the first thing. The only thing you have to do now. Foot striking the mattress on your way to the bookshelf, jarring the body, calm down. Can't. Hands fast through the stack, all the books about P., about saints, where did you put it, the one Peter lent you, jokingly calling it his "bible," the only book on the shelf with a spine in green, not gold: *Ecodefense*. Eyes hungry on the pages: the words are everywhere, the ones you are looking for, see? Back against the mattress, the light crawling over your lap, the photographs of forests, the diagrams, the instructions, the very short list. Of what you will require. A hand. A hammer. A nail.

He calls Jo before he remembers that she and Leni are out of town, somewhere in Florida for a family reunion Jo's dad insisted she attend, Leni tagging along, they'd made a collective gagging noise but went anyway and now no ride to the meeting, he has to take his bike, thirty-five miles, legs dead by the time he arrives. Breathless at the bottom of the steps, someone with blond dreads glancing at him, Lakota or Lakita or whatever her name is. Dang, did you run here or what? No, Xie says, I just need to talk to Peter, is he here? Rubbing his face with the cuff of his hoodie. Lakota shrugs. He's on the phone. Xie glances around the room. Fewer people than the last time he was here. No snacks, no tea. A thick crack in the concrete floor, where a rug used to be. What happened? he asks. Lakota smirks. Didn't you hear? And Peter materializing at his elbow, hand on Xie's back, Hey, farmer. What's going on? Xie asks. We're losing the space. Someone complained about drugs in the bathroom. Which weren't even ours. They told me today that they're canceling our lease. Smiling through his anger. I'm sorry, Xie says. Peter shrugs. We'll find somewhere. We always do. What did you need? Xie hands him a scrap of paper torn from the book. Peter unfolds it. Eyebrows up. How many? I don't know, a lot. Ten boxes, maybe more. Peter folds up the paper, puts it in his pocket. When do you need them by? Just, um. As soon as you can. Peter nods. No problem. Soft slap of Xie's arm. I'll drop them by your house. If you have a minute, we were just gonna talk about the situation in Alabama. The what? The coal project. Oh, I—I can't stay, I have to go. You sure? Alias mentioned you might be interested. Xie flushes. I'm—I am, but, I have to— Twitch of Peter's brow, impatient, I'm just asking for fifteen minutes, Xie. It's important. Xie rubs his head with both hands, anxious breath, shaky, I'm sorry, I just. Suddenly on the verge of tears. I have to run. Peter touching his arm. Hey, what's wrong? Xie shaking his head, emphatic, Nothing, I just—I really have to go. Peter drops his hand. Okay. I'm sorry, Xie says again, turning to flee, quick jog up the stairs, out the door, Peter's eyes at his back.

An hour home, mouth dry on the dark roads. Walking his bike through the birch. All the things that make their homes in the wood, the birds, the foxes, the rabbits, the deer, the primrose, the fern, that helpless army, do they know when something is coming, even before it is here? Do they pray? What is the afterlife of a tree slaughtered by a human. A sheet of paper. A table. The beam of a house. A smooth polished bowl, from which the murderers eat their soup.

He spends the day in the woods, starting from one end and walking to the other, back and forth, then weaving through on a diagonal, keeping the line as tight as possible, if you fuck it up start over. Testing himself. If I'm standing right here, do I know, in all directions, where I am. Clusters of crowns. Where the gaps are. Like animals, trees look the same when you aren't really looking; he looks now. With his hands, his eyes, his ears. Where the traffic is, on what road, the sounds from the house, the light from the church. The sun can tell you, the sky, the stars, the map is full of markers; fallen logs, fox dens, rabbit burrows, clusters of ferns, moss on the stones. Pattern upon pattern. To the east the land rises, just a little; to the west, it dips, you can feel the slope, so slight, beneath your feet. Eventually, even without using the stream or the church or the road for reference, keeping his eyes on the ground, he can orient himself, seeing in his mind the wood in all directions, from any point: I know you. The thrill of it; he slaps the side of the broken birch, the dead center of the wood, and whoops as the sun sinks through the trees until it is gone, the kingdom of the birch burning in the dark.

Erik, Jo, Leni, and Karen in the dining room, waiting for him at the kitchen table. Surprise. Leni's idea; she smiles, hopeful proud eyes, and he smiles back, shocked to see Karen in his house, a touch of lipstick, hair twisted back in a clip. Erik stands at the kitchen sink, drinking coffee. Wow, Xie says, plucking a leaf from his sleeve; you guys didn't have to do this. We made you a cake, Jo says. Coconut. We used beet juice for the dye, says Leni, so it's going to taste a little funny if you eat the frosting. Xie rubbing his brow. Um. Thanks. Erik cuts vegan pizzas and Leni opens bottles of ginger beer. Xie sits. Cheers, says Karen, and they touch bottles. So how old are you? Karen asks. He smiles. Sixteen. How old are you. She guffaws. Rude! Why's it rude for you and not for me? She rolls her eyes. I'm twenty-eight. Jo whistles. Leni pushes a plate toward Karen. Sorry it's all vegetables, Xie says, and Karen shakes her head. Looks delicious. How was Miami? he asks the girls; Jo's big sigh as she frees a piece of bell pepper from its sleeve of fake cheese. The ocean was red. Like, literally fucking *red* from that crazy algae they have growing down there, and my dad was trying to think of how, like, his company could purify it, you know, with their stupid machines, like the Gulf is just one big fucking faucet. We had to be like, um, no, that's not how it works, but he is constitutionally incapable of *getting* it. Leni shudders. What would help? Karen asks. Well, for starters, the complete dismantling of capitalism, probably, Jo says, and Karen smiles, wry. Right. Erik watching, silent as they talk. Xie wonders what he thinks of their little party, a messed-up teacher and two of the least-liked girls at MacAdams. Maybe he's pleased Xie has any friends at all, his father also a loner, so. How can he judge. If it's sad for Xie it's sad for all of them. But why think of any of it as sad. When he loves them all. Leni pushing a plastic bag across the table, Sorry I didn't wrap it but you don't believe in wrapping paper anyway, right? Xie wiping his mouth on his cuff. Pulls a book from the bag. *Becoming Biocentric: A Guide to Rejecting Anthropocentrism.* Open it, Leni urges. He does. *To Xie, a Hero for the Earth. Keep fighting. X Nova.* Xie grins. Karen leaning to read the title. Can I see? Xie sliding the book to her. We've been reading it and it's *so* good, Jo says. It's been out for a couple of years but the information is still super-relevant. Erik uncrossing his arms. How about cake, he says. P. polishing his boots with the hem of his cape in the corner. Pancratius never made it to sixteen. Make a wish. The lights suddenly out and everyone. Singing. Erik lifting the cake over Xie's head, tall yellow candles lit. All the faces at the table illuminated, watching him. Smell of coconut. Of smoke. What should I wish. Blows the candles out but for a moment a light, still, in the dark, before the lamp is switched back on.

After FKK leaves he walks Karen to her car. Thanks for coming, he says. My pleasure. They're really sweet girls. And your dad is nice, too. Sorry he doesn't talk much, Xie says. Karen smirks. Apple doesn't fall far from the tree, she says. Dropping a small velveteen bag into his palm. What's this? She shrugs. Present. He pinches the bag between his fingers. Pouring a necklace into his palm. Silver medal. A boy in a field, arm aloft. *St. Pancratius pray for us.* He's the patron saint of young people, right? she says. Teresa'd be more obvious, but. He's a local. Xie's smile as he puts it over his head, tucking it beneath his hoodie. I love it. I'm glad, Karen says. Make sure you eat more of that cake, yeah? You're getting skinny. Patting his side. Last smile before getting into her car. When he goes back into the house his father is at the table, elbows spread, leafing through Nova's book. You know this person? I met her once, Xie says. A few months ago. Met her where? Xie hesitates. At a, um, environmental activism thing. In town? Yeah. Erik frowns. I don't seem to know much about how you spend your time, he says. Turning a page: What to Do If You're Arrested. If you plan on doing something stupid, I hope you'll warn me. We can't afford another surprise. Closing the book. Xie quiet, gripping the back of a chair. Why do you assume that I'd do something stupid? I don't, I just—all I want is for you to try. Try what? To just. Be happy. Erik looks at him, steady. Long silence. I am, Xie says. I'm trying. P. opposite his father, very bright. Taking more and more of the room, as if. Marking his territory. Almost all of it, now, his, and Erik in a sliver of shadow. Xie starts to gather the dishes but Erik rises, puts a hand on his shoulder to stop him. Let me do it. Taking Karen's plate from his hand. Your mother sent a card, he says. It's on the table. Xie opens it. A hundred-dollar bill and a card with a dog wearing a birthday hat. *Hope you have a barking good time. Love, Mommy*. He rips the card in half. Folds the pieces into the trash. His father filling the sink with water. Did Karen talk to you? Xie asks. Mm. What did she say? Erik dips a plate into the water. She told me what I already know. Xie frowns. What, that I'm not doing what Mac-Adams wants me to do? That I fuck everything up? His father's elbow working in a circle as he scrubs. No, he says. That you are extraordinary.

Two days later Peter at the door. Hey. Fingers deep in his beard. Scratching. Hey, Xie says, and lets himself be hugged, Peter slapping his back, it's not so bad but. Someone could tell him he could maybe slap a little less hard. Got your stuff, Peter says. Xie helps bring the boxes into the garden, stacking them beneath a tarp next to the compost. Both of them panting, midafternoon and strangely warm, sun hot off the white sides of the house. Xie lifts a flap of cardboard. Six-inch silver nails packed together head to tail. Sledgehammer with a gleaming gold head. If this isn't enough I can get more. Just let me know. No, this is good. It's great. Thank you, Xie says, digging in his pocket. Offering the hundred-dollar bill his mother sent. We have a donor, Peter says, shaking his head. They're free. Xie still holding the bill out. Just, take it. Please. Use it for whatever you want. Rent for a new space, or. Whatever. You sure? Yeah. Peter takes the bill, tucks it into his back pocket. Circles the garden. Nice setup out here, he says. Thumbing the leaves of the leeks. You left in such a hurry the other day. I was worried about you. Xie chewing his lip. I'm fine. I talked about Alabama with FKK. We're going. Peter lifts his head, sudden smile. Yeah? What about your probation? Xie shrugs. Doesn't matter. Peter's grin widens. That's awesome. Glad we can count on you. Xie nods. Anytime. Peter looks out across the stream. Both of them watching the woods. They're gorgeous, Peter says. Yeah, Xie says. They are. First buds on the branches. You know what you're doing, right? Xie nods. Peter's sideways look. You got help? A breeze strokes the birch. P. leaning against a trunk, silver on silver. Yeah, Xie says. I have help. Peter nods, hand again on his shoulder. Well. Good luck, farmer. And he goes.

The first night it rains. Lightning cutting lavender into the clouds. He has his pack, the hammer, the nails. Gloves. A blade to make his mark. Savage sound of water pound-

ing the roof. In the attic it's so loud. He waits. Sitting beside
the body. Skull on the pillow. Eyes always seeing. Something. What. Dark pools. Blow after blow of thunder. The
light in the window. P. with his crown against the glass.
Chin on Xie's knee, cape pooled against the floor. Midnight. One. The rain stops. The clouds melt beneath the
stars.

A hundred trees a night. Three nails to a tree. Starting
at the north end and working in rows, left to right. He
strokes the first damp trunk. His forehead against the bark.
The nail pulled from his pack, cold through the gloves:
Start at the top. Hold it at an angle. Cocks his arm. Fingers
trembling so hard he drops the nail once, twice, bending
to feel for it in the dark, wiping his head on his sleeve,
please god help me. Holding his breath. P. behind him.
Steadying his arm. Bring it down, three times, the nail
only halfway through. Now it is the tree that trembles.
Lift the hammer again. Clip the head of the nail with
the bolt cutters, catching the knob of metal in his fist.
The nail flush with the flesh of the tree. Beloved. Kneel
at the base. Make the mark, fresh *X* just above the root.
And then up, to the next tree, the moon slipping down
through the trunks, dim, dimmer, cold sweat beneath
his hoodie, hands wet beneath the gloves, the flesh of the
birch much harder than he imagined, the nail squealing
through inch by inch, the head of the hammer stutter-
ing across the bark when he misses. Pain from shoulder
to knuckle, relentless, he is drunk with it by the fiftieth

tree. It hurts them, too, he knows. Don't flinch. I love you. I'm sorry. His arm burning all through the flesh, the bone, deep ache in his elbow, in his back, dropping nails when his fingers go numb, fumbling with the pack, losing his grip on the bolt cutters, can't close his hand, blistered skin turned to jelly. He laughs, weeping, he had no idea how weak he was, how fucking useless. Sunk on his knees in the mud. You'll never do it. You stupid crazy idiot you'll never get them all and if anything happens to them it's your fault. Get up. P. says, but Xie stays on his knees, hands loose at his sides, I can't. P.'s hand in his hair, wrenching his head up. Holds it. Look. And there, against the white bark of the tree before him, a perfect line of blood, falling from crown to root. No sound. No light. There is no P. The wet trunk. Can't hear himself breathe. The blood is slow, too slow, endless, he knows it will keep coming, calm, inevitable, reflected in all the silver in the air, slow motes of dust, of ash, and the smell of burning: am I a tree now, too? Am I

Or do you think there is a sign where there is no sign

The next morning early to the library, gritty eyed, the night before spent huddled against the body, unable to think, to sleep, bandaged hands curled against his chest. Karen's car in the parking lot, engine running. He waits on the steps. She doesn't come out. Two minutes. Five. He goes to the car, leans to look through the window.

Her head on the wheel, hair obscuring her face. Hesitant knock on the glass. No answer. Says her name. Karen. Are you okay. The car unlocked, so. Go around. Opens the passenger door. Blast of heat and the smell of her so strong inside. Sweet over something sour. Her arm hanging limp at her side. What if. Dead or. But no, some sound coming from her, mumbling. What? Karen, it's me, are you. And touching her arm, she lifts her head, what is that other smell. Realizing. Drunk. One kind of panic replaced by another. Here, can you sit up? Her head falling back, mouth open, she swallows. Squints. But can't. Talk. Did you drive like this? No bottle in the car, but. A thermos in the cupholder. Sniffs it. Pure alcohol. Shit, he breathes. Her heavy exhale, unintelligible murmur. The parking lot not. Safe because. She could get in trouble or. Fired, if Greg finds out, reports her. Hand still on her arm to keep her from flopping over. Her cheek creased from the wheel. All that trash on the floor, clothes and plastic bags strewn over the backseat. Am I supposed to know what to do tell me what to do. Keys in the ignition. Drive her somewhere. Home. Glance at the library door and then. Kneeling on the seat, lean to grab her beneath the arms and slide her to the passenger side, legs catching on the center console, Xie pushing at her thigh, Karen can you. Move. Her eyes finally seeing him. Xie? Sharp movement of her head forward, almost clipping his nose. Xie panting. Yeah, it's me. Fuck, she mumbles. Closes her eyes. He grits his teeth, hefting both her legs across the console, her shoe popping off her heel. Backs of her knees damp through her jeans, who knows how long she sat here with the heat on. Flesh slack in his arms, helpless. Settles her into the seat, pulls the belt across her hip. Her head sliding toward the window as he is about to close the door, he has to push her back, hard, shut the door and into the driver's seat. Looks over the dashboard, slaps the heat off, hand trembling, wiping his face, quick, Okay, he says to himself, okay, putting his foot on the brake as he turns the key in the ignition. The car throbbing to life. Can't manage reverse so eases forward. Slow through the intersection then. Up past the woods. Karen trying to fish a hair from her mouth. Please don't move until we stop. On the incline has to. Press the gas. The car darts forward, almost missing a curve. Xie yelps. Death grip on the steering wheel, blisters screaming beneath the gauze. He keeps one foot on the brake the whole time. Almost there. Half a rabbit on the yellow line, bright blood on white fur. Don't look. Finally his driveway and he puts the car in park, askew, keys out, deep breath. Goes to her door. She reaches one leg out for the ground as if unsure where exactly it is. Heavy lurch onto her feet. His arm around her waist, stiff jacket beneath his hand. Brushing her hair out of his own face. Stumble over the doorstep. Shuffle to the couch. Here, he says. Karen half sits, half rests her head on the arm. Eyes closed. Dry swallow. He gets her a glass of water, a blanket, helps her drink, takes off her shoes. Why did she get so fucked up at ten in the morning. Trying to remember, did I ever smell alcohol on her before? But sure this is the first time. And her driving like this. Or did she start drinking in the parking lot or. Fuck's sake,

Karen. She's not asleep but trying to be still. Lets her be.
Boils water in the kitchen. Makes tea. Quiet. Strong sun
through the window, bright square on her hip. Watching
her. Such silence. He sits at the table, Nova's book open,
eyes restless on the page and eventually she falls asleep
and when she awakes she seems. Better. Blinking, quick
turn of her head, Xie—? He gets up from the table. Yeah.
She sits, folding the blanket over the back of the couch,
clumsy, as if she can't quite feel her hands. How did I get
here? Um. I drove. You drove? Yeah, you were in your car,
so. I, um. Drove it. Here. She turns her head from the
light and he pulls the curtain across the window. May
I use your bathroom. Voice flat, quiet. He shows her and
she shuts the door. Running water. He makes toast. After ten minutes she comes out, face scrubbed, her hair in
a ponytail. Sits at the table, where he has put her toast,
a jar of jam, tea. She eats. Tiny bites of bread. Squints
into the tea, steam crawling up her cheeks. Xie scratching his neck. Do you want to see the garden? Karen looks
up, blank. Then nods. Knuckles white around the mug.
Okay. He leads her to the yard. Stepping down into the
dirt. Her hand shading her eyes. Walking around the
boxes. Fingering the kale. If there's anything you want I
can. Put it in a bag for you, he says. Breath steaming. Her
brow furrowed, brushing the tops of the beets. I could
take some of these, she says. Xie pulls them up. Brisk rub
of dirt from the skins. What happened to your hand? she
says. He winces. Nothing. Karen going over the garden as
if judging a science fair project, little frown. You've done
so much. He shrugs. I have a lot of time. She points to

a bunch of kale and he pulls that up, too. She rubs her arms. What are these, she says, jutting her chin toward a purple petal near the fence. Hellebore, he says. Isn't it early for flowers? Not these. They don't mind the cold. They're pretty, she says. Yeah. His sleeve touching hers. She pulls away, holding her arm to her chest. Hard mud climbing the sides of her shoes. Well, she says. She goes up the steps, opens the screen door. In the kitchen he puts the vegetables in a box, adds a jar of jam, a handful of mushrooms. She folds the blanket, takes her mug and plate to the sink. He carries the box to her car, sets it on the passenger seat. Karen waits at the other door, tucking a shredded tissue beneath her nose. Do you have the keys, she says. He takes them from his pocket, puts them in her hand. Thank you. Eyes never meeting his. Why would she come to the library if she. Didn't want someone to find her. Him to find her. He goes into the house. His father not home until late so stay in bed. Chin on skull. Arm over rib. The body is never cold, never really warm. Will she make it home okay. Will she hate me for knowing. What do I know. That she is sad? That she is alone? That she started drinking and then couldn't stop. At ten in the morning. Needing it that much. The way he needs the body, long fuck before the woods, no dinner, then out to the trees, three hours, then back in bed, sleepless, it hurts to touch the body but he does it anyway, again and again, and while he dreams of the body there are men dreaming of swallowing the woods.

———

He knows, through the nails, so much more about the birch. Their skin like the cortical layer of bone, hard but porous, rough and smooth, their white that is really gray, yellow, brown, black, full of all the pits and wounds a living thing sustains. The nail slicing though time, ring after ring, pinning the first moment to this, him to the heart. Sneakers soft in the undergrowth. The eyes of the wrens on him, the gray fox, the mule deer, barred owl, Appalachian cottontail, they all know him now, the sound of Xie, the sound of the hammer on the nail. Half foe. The most vital portion of the wood hidden underground, arterial, billions of miles of microscopic fungal filaments connecting each tree to its others, thousands of roots binding earth to stone. You walk right over it. It is what allows you to walk at all. One tree to the next. And between them an invisible net, mineral, chemical, aqueous, photonic, that binds them to one another, you to them. The wood is alive. It knows how to live.

Waiting for FKK to take him to the next meeting. A black car he's never seen pulls up in the driveway. Jo rolls the window down, holds out an arm. Hey whore, she says. Bet you couldn't hear me coming. He stands, brushing his hands on his hips. What happened to your car? he asks. She grins. I sold it. Slapping the shiny door with her palm. Plug 'n' play, bitches. Inside, the smell of plastic and microfiber and Jo's new earthy scent, she doesn't smoke anymore and washes her hair with what looks like a bar of soap, infused with hemp, Leni gave him some once and

Erik took one sniff and said, Dear god. The new car weirdly quiet. When did you get it? This morning, Jo beams. It's the first one in the county. I had to order it three months ago. Oh, Xie says. Blisters itchy on his palms, he hides them in his cuffs. They turn down roads he's never seen, pavement turning to dirt, lightless except for the car. Are you sure you know where you're going? Leni asks. Yes, Mother, Jo replies, because *I* know how to read a *map*. The headlights suddenly hit the white sides of a partially demolished three-story house. Something out of a horror film: broken glass, graffiti, whole walls missing and something green growing out of one side. Holy fuck, Leni whispers. It's fine, Jo says. Leni doesn't move. I said it's *fine*. Leni sliding in slow motion from the car. In one of the rooms on the first floor the strong smell of weed and sweat, a younger crowd with intense eyes and cagey posture, a few familiar to Xie but most of them strangers, no Peter, though they all seem to know Jo and she slips among them as cool as he has ever seen her, slapping hands, chin tipped, Leni at her elbow, trying to hide her overbite by pushing her jaw out, turning to beckon Xie but he doesn't follow. Suddenly tired, stuck, old bad feeling in his guts, what am I doing here. Wasting time. He circles back through what used to be a kitchen, great holes in the blackened linoleum showing straight through to a dirt basement. In the front room a cat paces in a figure eight, interior walls stripped to the studs, trash and old paint and sawdust littering the floor and every window broken open onto the night. Various species of shit petrified in the corners. Candles stuck in their own wax. The cat brushes its nose against his hand and he touches its back. Dozens of people spread throughout the house, footsteps overhead, Xie waiting for them to fall through the ceiling, careful to stay away from the center of the room. The cat threading between his legs and the wall. A girl comes in, alone, her eyes nervous around the room before meeting his, long blond hair from beneath a black beanie, tights and black velvet skirt, black jean jacket. He blinks. Hey, she says, I'm looking for Justin? Xie opens his mouth, closes it, opens it again. Sorry, I don't really know anyone around here. Little laugh at his own stupidity but she just nods, serious. Oh, well, that's okay. Glancing again around the room. This place doesn't seem super-safe. She reaches to pet the cat but it darts off before she can get her hands on it. Dusts her palms against her ass. This is a big group for the area, she says. There's a university nearby, he says, E.A. started there, so. It's like a hub, I heard. She squints. Are you from California? He nods. Me, too, she says. Berkeley. You look kind of familiar, did you do any work out there? No, I. Just started coming to these a year ago. I wasn't that active in California. A pause. Hey, he says, sinking his fists into the pocket of his hoodie. Do you know, um, Nova, by any chance? The girl pushes her lips to the side. You mean the founder of Earth Alliance? Yeah, he says. I just. Wondered if you knew where she was, or. How to get a hold of her. No, sorry, the girl says, tucking her hair beneath her beanie. But someone here must, right? If you ask around? Yeah, Xie says, chin to his chest. Yeah, probably. A guy in a huge green army jacket comes in, spots

the girl. Well, it was nice to meet you, she says, as Justin
puts his arm around her neck, pulls her head to his lips
for a kiss. Laughter beneath the window. Glass shattering
against something upstairs, someone's whoop, footsteps
thumping down the staircase. Wishes Peter would show
up but knows he won't, the vibe of this place too dark for
him, revolving around some fractured purpose that
seems intentionally exclusionary, no community food table or sign-up sheets or chairs in a circle, just these bleakly
intense pockets of activity, urgent but stalled at the same
time. It's like being in his own head, but worse. The cat
reappears and puts its paws on his leg. What do you want,
he says. It meows. He picks it up, careful, and takes it to
the front steps, the cat purring rustily in his lap. A circle
of girls smoking, casting incurious glances at Xie from
the corners of their eyes. A boy in bright white Converse
stalking out onto the porch, launching past Xie into the
dirt, pursued by a trio of other boys trying to calm him.
Man, chill, just chill! And the angry one turning on
them, hard, arms up, Are you fucking *hearing* me? It *used*
to be you needed *clearance* to come to these things, only
people with a rep could join but now it's a goddamn free-
for-all, assholes are posting locations on fucking *Facebook*, how am I supposed to trust any of you bastards?
Turning his eyes to Xie, the cat jumping away. I mean,
who is this punk, huh, you come here and just fucking
stare at shit, I mean who the fuck *are* you, how do I know
you're not working for the— Leni, from nowhere, heavy
step across the rotting porch, Xie would not have believed
someone as small as her could make her body so loud,

getting right up in the guy's face, yelling, Back *up*, and the guy trying to get past her but she doesn't move, following his body with her own, holding his gaze even though she is shaking so hard her teeth chatter, why does she think she has to protect him, defend him? He wants to show them his hands, wants to shout, How do you know what I do? What I think? How I feel? If they want all this to themselves they can have it and he is off, like always, out to the car alone. Leni running up to his side, God, he's so stupid, just ignore him. Xie's furious shrug. He's right. I don't know why I even bother coming to this shit. Leni's hand on his sleeve; he pulls away. Don't be like that, Xie. Everyone wants you here. Xie stops short, incredulous. Everyone? Really? Leni's helpless gray eyes wide, vein pulsing in her skinny neck. How weak she looks, is, always at Jo's side, like a dog. She takes a step back, quick, as if seeing the thought in his face. He looks away, flushing. I'll wait. Okay, she says, turning to go back to the house, holding her elbows. Xie ducking through the branches to the car, yanking open the back door. Lies in the back. Fucking new car. P. nowhere. Fuck you, too. Closing his eyes only to hear, a moment later, the door wrenched open, Jo jamming herself into the front seat. Leaning to look out the window, heavy sigh, heave back out to kick a skateboard away from the car, shouting, Would you clear your shit out of the way, Amber! Then back in and the door slammed twice, spinning out onto the narrow road. You need to grow a pair, Xie, you can't let people talk to you like that. Xie sitting up, slow. What does it matter to you what anyone says. Jo's snort. Excuse me? What do you want me to do, let you get your ass kicked? Xie rolling his eyes, Leni was the first one out, you were too busy holding court— Holding court? You mean doing our job? You're right, that's exactly what I was *too busy* doing, while you were sitting off in some fucking *corner*— Leni saying, quiet, Come on, Jo, he's shy. I know he's fucking *shy*, Leni, Jesus, everyone's shy, it's no excuse for acting like a sociopath. Xie flinging his arm in the air, Why do you even invite me then, you're always off with those—people we don't even *know*. Jo's hard laugh, You mean *you* don't know them, because you don't *want* to know them. Those people aren't the bad guys, Xie, there's a whole community right here, people who want the same things you want, people who are willing to do the work that you always *say* you want to do, so what the hell is your problem? Xie glances at her in the mirror. Silence. Jo's eyes meeting his. What. Xie shrugging. Nothing. What's that look mean? What look. Xie shifting in his seat, the smell of the microfiber seats and the plastic dashboard noxious, he needs air, fumbling with the buttons on the handle of the door, but they're locked; Jo has to press something up front before the window will go down. You know my dad spent hours converting the engine for you on the Jetta and it was running fine, he says, staring hard out the window. Oh, so *that's* what this is about. Okay. What do you want to say, Mr. Perfect? I'm not perfect, I just—electricity still— And Jo nodding, angrily, Mm-hm, yes, electricity *what*? Xie gesturing with both hands, At least with the oil we were reusing something that was going to be thrown away, it wasn't even an

old car and you just went out and bought another one
like, why, you don't— Xie, that thing was smoking every
morning and it's fucking useless in the winter, every time
I got in the car I was worried the fucking thing was going
to *explode*. I'm grateful for your dad's help but it's *my
fucking car* which *you* are happy enough to ride around in
everywhere, so— And Xie raising his voice, But I'm *not*
happy, I *hate* driving, I wouldn't even— You what, you
wouldn't stoop to being in a vehicle if it wasn't for us
forcing you into one? No, just—forget it. Jo scoffs. No, go on,
I'm loving this, really. Xie shakes his head, I said for*get* it,
okay, and Jo wrenches the car to the shoulder, all of their
heads slamming forward as she hits the brakes. A sudden
silence. Get out, Jo says. He blinks. Leni's head dipped,
eyeing them both warily, like someone used to arguments
turning bad, and he wonders, do they hit her at home or
does she see someone getting hit? Jo opening his door
and taking him by the arm, yanking him onto the road.
Come on. Xie stepping back, Jesus, Jo, I'm not going to
fight you. I don't mean that, you idiot, I mean just *say* it!
Xie's hands up. It's your car, fine, you can do what you
want, and Jo shaking her head. You want everything and
everyone to be so pure and anyone who does something
you don't like you just fucking *judge*. I can't even *handle*
watching you stare at anyone who tries to talk to you as if
they have a fucking *disease* because they're smoking a
Marlboro or—or—fucking have gel in their hair or whatever it is you find so offensive about the entire human
race. Leni staring through the glass. Shivering. Sitting
around in your room making lentil soup and riding your

bike downtown doesn't make you a fucking saint, okay? Xie frowns. I didn't say it did. Jo throwing up her hands. But that's how you act! Like you know so much more than every fucking—oh my god, there are so many people here—who do so much more than you could ever *dream* of doing, who risk their *lives*, who get thrown in fucking *jail*— Stopping at Xie's sharp look. Is that it? You're still pissed that you got caught and we didn't? Xie's flinch, What? No— Jo continuing, You think we should have stayed with you? Do you know what would have happened if Leni got caught out there? Xie confused, glancing through the window at Leni, who looks at her lap, hair hanging in her face. Her dad's friends with Moore, okay, he would kill her if he knew what she was doing. She doesn't have a family like yours, they're not going to just smile and nod and pay for her fucking rice milk, they don't even know she's vegan, that she's queer, they don't want to know anything about her, and you want to walk around like everything is so *hard* for you, you suffer so much, everyone else is some clueless asshole, when you don't even know what life is like for your so-called best friends, okay? I'm sorry, Xie stutters, I didn't know— Because you never *ask*! she shouts. He looks at the pavement, shatter of glass from an accident on the white line. I'm sorry, he says. I'm just. I'm sorry. Not knowing how to explain it, how far away he feels, a feeling he doesn't know how to fix. Jo rubs her wrist against her brow. Drops her arms at her sides. We love you, okay. Just. Don't be such an ass. He looks at her. Yeah, he says. Okay. She takes his arm. Come on, you idiot. He climbs back in. Xie's body weirdly sore, like he has been hit. All over. Leni turning the radio on, which for some reason is tuned to a country station but no one says anything, they just listen to Willie Nelson and Tim McGraw for ten minutes. Windows cracked. Parking at Leni's favorite vegan diner. My treat, Jo says. He goes to the bathroom to wash his hands and the light is so dim he thinks he sees blood. Doesn't. Does. Holding his fingers to his face. Panic beating a distant drum. Thinking: You're fine. P. there to touch his palms, helmet bent to kiss them, there is all night ahead of them, still. So much to do. The girls are in the car with cashew milkshakes and fries and he eats, mechanically, while they play a game Leni invented called *Who's Fucking Who*. A woman goes in with her Chihuahua under her arm. *Definitely* fucking, Jo says, and they laugh, Xie loudest of all. What does any of it mean. Try to see yourself from the outside. Are you. Just a person or a fucking clown?

The next two nights are dry; he drags himself through the woods in a trance, P. at his side: he thinks nothing, feels nothing. Hammer, nail, birch, bone. The pain comes later. Wrapping his hand at the kitchen sink in the morning, bubble of peroxide, Erik angling to look. What happened? I cut it, Xie says, pulling away. It's fine. Erik watching him, knowing something. Not enough. In the evenings pulling out the deck of cards but Xie can't hold them without shaking, he pretends he is tired, goes to wait in the attic for his father to fall asleep. The math is unrelenting: a night, an hour, even a dozen trees off means some of them might go unspiked and you don't know. Where they will cut first. He rests in the woods. Cheek on the dirt. Shallow cradle in the earth, dug with his hands, just long enough to curl up in. Warmer down here. Hood pulled tight around his head. Such smells, toward morning, when the air gets thicker with dew, dense perfume: mineral, loam, feather, all varieties of shit, dead meat, skunk, flower, mushroom, mold. Missing the body. Does it miss him? You have to be willing. P. blows the leaves from his shoulder, settles over him, cutting out the sky. Heavy. Face against his. He can see, inside the dark hollows of his eyes, where the tiny fingernail-sized lacrymal bones should be, slim vertical ridges along which tears make their way to the surface of a face. The body has these bones, he has touched them many times, but the bones inside P.'s face are completely smooth. P.'s fingers sliding over the bridge of Xie's nose, beneath his eye. Beloved. Don't cry.

He's afraid Karen won't show, Friday, in the library, but there she is, on time, her head bent over her notebook, the sleeves of her jacket pushed to her elbows. Fine red hair on her arms. Morning, she says, gaze even, as careful as he is not to betray embarrassment. He sits. Trying not to yawn. Morning. Karen scratches a bad pen against her paper, sighs, digs in her bag for a new one. Mascara thickening the corners of her pale lashes. Who does she put that poison on for? Or is it to hide something, like his hood, a mask, don't look at me. She spreads her hands over her notebook and he sees that there are little white spots on the cuffs of her jacket where there used to be dark marks, the blue fibers frayed as if she had scrubbed them with a stiff brush. He looks at a textbook but his eyes won't stay open; now that he knows she's okay exhaustion hits him like a brick. Xie, she says. He straightens. Mm. Mouth dry. He rubs it on his sleeve. Did you get any sleep? A little, he mumbles. Palming the side of his face. Feels the hammer in his hand. Hammer a part of him. The smell of the woods on his clothes, does she notice? Karen taps his wrist with her pen. Drink some water, she says. He pushes up from the chair, drags to the fountain, drinks, comes back. They look at each other. So, she says. What are we doing today. He shrugs. I meant to bring that book FKK got me but I forgot it at home. Have you read it? Some of it, yeah. Well, when you remember to bring it I'd be happy to look at it with you. A silence. She rubs her neck. He puts his head on his outstretched arm and she nudges it with her elbow. He grunts, sits up. Why so sleepy, hm, she says. Busy, he says. With what? With stuff, he says, head tipped back to the ceiling, staring at the water stains there. Did you like school, he asks. Karen shrugs. In a way. It was something I knew how to do. Kind of the opposite of you. But did you believe in it? Believe in it in what way? That it was good or. Worth your time. She snorts. I would say it was an entirely amoral practice, Xie. It was what I could do so I did it. Xie looks at her. Smiles. Pretty lame coming from a teacher. Well, I'm the worst teacher and you're the worst student, so. We're even. They sit. Can we go for a walk? he says. Where? I don't know. Shrugs. Woods? he suggests. What woods? He nods his head in the direction of the birch. She checks her watch. Sighs. Sure, why not. They leave their things on the table. Greg watching them go. She zips her jacket to the neck even though it's sixty degrees out. Why are you always so cold? he asks, and she looks surprised. I'm not. Light wind lifting her hair. They cross the empty intersection and turn up the road that curves sharply toward the trees. You know I talked to your father, she says. I thought the school might do it eventually anyway and I just wanted to get out in front of it. They turn off the tarmac into the woods, stepping over the guardrail. He had pried the PRIVATE PROPERTY signs from the trees weeks before and the pale spots where the signs had been still show. He knows you're doing good work with me, and he knows MacAdams isn't seeing any of it. Their feet hit the soft earth at the same time. And there is P., stepping with them, not at Xie's side but hers. Some animal darts from the hollow, brown body quick through the undergrowth. The school is going to want to meet with you at some point, and me, and your father. You don't have to go. But they will expel you eventually. She looks up at the birch. He's on your side, she says. Like me. Xie nods. The handle of P.'s sword taps her hip, that's how close he is walking to her. She takes a baggie of celery from her pocket, offers it to him; he declines. Where do you go, he asks. What do you mean? Like when you want to hang out or whatever. She chews, thinking. I don't know. I like being at home, I guess. I'm definitely not out in the woods, if that's what you mean. But you grew up here, in the country, right? She shrugs. Yeah, but I guess it never really rubbed off on me, the whole outdoors thing. She peels a string off a piece of celery. Wipes it on her thigh. But you, you came all this way from the city. To live *here*. Of all places. You don't think it's beautiful? Of course it's beautiful. But I always feel like it doesn't have anything to do with me. Like it doesn't want me. What doesn't? Karen sucks the end of her celery, brows knit. Nature. She steps over a cracked branch, her hand steady on a trunk, following him. They walk. My dad doesn't like it here, Xie says. No? No. I mean, I think he just, um. Misses blending in a bit more. Him blending in, or you? Both, I guess. Squinting. Well, it's just been a couple of years, right? That's not that long. It takes a while to find where you fit in. A little pause. She watches him. But this is your place, isn't it? Yeah, he says. Quiet. Fern brushing his shin. But I don't know if it's enough. Enough for what? He shrugs. Doesn't answer. She puts the baggie back in her pocket, swallows the last of the celery. Brushing the knee of her jeans. They are almost at the center of the woods. Light in thick ropes running between the trees, turning the dust in the air to gold. He watches her face as they approach the church, the abrupt limit of the woods giving way to grass. The strange sudden beauty of it in all that green. She stops, lips parted. Gazing at it. Weeds long against its sides. Bronze bell motionless in its little tower. You want to go in? he asks. She blinks. Deep breath. I guess, yeah. Gesturing for him to lead the way through the grass to the steps. Inside it is cool, damp, slight smell of mold. She looks around. The doors have been removed from P.'s case, glass restored, only the sword remaining inside. So this is where he was, she says, stroking the gold hinge. Reading the prayer on the paper tacked to the glass. *I believe, Heavenly Father, all that Faith teaches, and in that faith I wish to live and die; O glorious St. Pancratius, I beg you, with all the affection of my heart, to teach us, especially the youth, with what courage we should flee from sin, so that, undefiled, I may live a holy life on earth and win eternal glory in Heaven, Amen.* And below it, handwritten: *Please pray for the return of our Saint.* Karen looks over her shoulder; Xie follows her gaze. P. at the door. What? Nothing, she says. Just feel like we're going to get in trouble or something. Scolded by a nun. Do you want to light a candle? he asks. She rubs her hands together, brisk. Yeah, let's do the candles. She digs in her coat pocket, puts a quarter in the donation box beneath the altar. Taking a candle from his hand, screwing the taper into the iron holder. Strike the long match. Now what. I don't know, he says. You don't have to do anything. He stares at the flame. Remembers how there was always a candle here, lit, when he came. Karen elbows him. Are you praying? He smiles. No. No? I'm just thinking. About what? He shrugs. They look at their flames. If only he could say, There is this person I love. And he's not even a person. After a moment Karen's quick breath. Do we blow them out or. No, I think you just let them burn. She gathers her hair, twists it, lets it go. He sniffs, breaking off a little arm of wax from the altar. Do you think you'd want to come sometime. With me and FKK. To, um. A protest. Her eyebrows high. Me? He nods. Yeah, she says, immediate. I would. I will. Without thinking he takes her hand, pulls it. To his mouth. Quick kiss on the knuckle. She laughs, squeezing his fingers. They take one last look at the church, straight up at the ceiling, its prim painted arches. Beautiful, she says. They walk back through the yellow grass together, P. leading the way back to the road, his sword dragging behind him, drawing a line in the dirt.

He spends two hours making a lentil loaf, rolls, mashed potatoes, and homemade gravy. His father home late and Xie just waits, patient, the food cold but it's worth it to see Erik's face, full of surprise at the linen tablecloth and old china, cloth napkins folded beneath the knives. What's all this. Shrug. Dinner. Looks nice, Erik says. Xie pouring water into tall glasses. Cheers. Cheers. Quick bite of the loaf dragged through the gravy. Eyebrows. It's good. Yeah, it's. From a recipe. What's the occasion? Xie clearing his throat. I had something to ask you. Erik pauses, then resumes eating. Oh? What's that? Xie pushes a forkful of potatoes from one end of his plate to the other. There's this protest. A silence, as if Erik hasn't heard, chewing. Then finally without looking up: A protest? Yeah, of. Um. It's in Alabama and. It's about. Mountaintop removal. They want to get rid of about, um, a million acres of. The land around there. So. A lot of people are going to protest next weekend. Erik nods. I heard about that, yeah. Silence. Erik glancing up. And you wanted to spend how long there? Just a couple days. I thought you might come with us. Erik pauses. Reaching to brush Xie's hair out of his eyes, flinching when Xie flinches. The girls are going? Xie nods. And Karen, I think. Erik ducking his head to his fork. Karen's into that sort of thing? It's not something people are "into," Dad, all kinds of people are going, like thousands and thousands of people. These companies, they're taking a hundred tons of coal out of the ground every two seconds, the land they want to use has the oldest and most diverse forests in the *country*. Erik splits a roll with his thumbs, packs in a knifeful of butter. You're still on probation. Yeah, but there's no rule about me going to a protest— Erik raising his hand. I'm just saying, you have to promise me it'll be safe. He pauses. Takes another bite of bread. And that I can do the driving. Xie grins, slapping his palms on the table. Deal.

Everyone meets at Xie's, Erik arranging their bags in the back of Jo's car. He doesn't say anything about the Jetta, or the bottles of oil thickening in the garage, untouched since winter. K, you got shotgun, Jo says. Karen's eyebrow at the nickname as she gets in. It's a good thing you two are fucking sticks, Jo mutters as she settles into her seat, Leni in the middle, thigh-to-thigh with Jo. Seat belts, Erik says. Jo passes her iPod up to the front. Erik's dim smile as he sets it in the cupholder. Driver chooses music, he says. Mr. L, are you going to be a total Nazi for six and a half hours? 'Cause I don't think I can handle, like, pure totalitarianism. Erik snorts. You'll live. Karen unfolding a map. Erik starting the car. I know the way, he says. Karen pauses, then folds the map back up. Tom Petty on the radio again. All the trees slipping past. So tell us more about this protest, Karen says. Sounds like a lot of people will be there. Jo nodding. There are thirty-two groups involved, officially. Monday they're going to start the mining, so some of the groups will stay in the camps, in between the land and the equipment. On the land that Century Energy owns? Karen asks. Won't the police just remove them? Well, they're going to be locked neck to neck, so it will take a really long time to get them all undone. Karen frowns. What do you mean? Jo leans forward, scrolling for a photo to show Karen on her phone. They use, like, bike locks? Literally they just lock themselves to each other at the neck and it takes forever for the cops to separate them in order to make arrests. That's intense, Karen says. Yeah, well, it's a million fucking acres of land, you know? We're really glad you came, by the way, Jo adds. It's cool that you guys would do this. Erik glances in the mirror. Xie made a compelling case, he says. Leni whispers something to Jo and Jo pulls her backpack onto her lap, unzipping it to reveal Tupperware filled with giant white squares. We made these last night, Leni says, passing the tub to the front. They're vegan Rice Krispies treats. Karen offers one to Erik. God, he says, grimacing through a mouthful, and Jo scoffs. What, they're amazing! Karen shrugs. I think they're great. Erik's elbow on the rolled-down window. Arm straight on the wheel. His close-cropped hair almost pure silver now. He was forty when Xie was born, already old. Karen starts a game of

Twenty Questions. Leni keeps forgetting if it's animal or vegetable and Jo yells at her to get with the program. They park at the motel, check in. Three rooms in a row. Xie and Erik, FKK, Karen on her own. Erik passing out the keys. Leni like a puppy, jumping down the hall, purple carpet on the walls. This place is a *trip*. Freaking out when Jo opens the door. You mean we get our own *bathroom*? and Jo saying, Leni, have you seriously never stayed in a motel before? Leni twirls. Nope. Jo rolls her eyes. Hillbilly. Erik asks what they want for dinner and FKK says, Pizza!! and when he looks confused Jo pulls a bottle of hot sauce from her bag and says, No cheese. They sit on FKK's bed and when the pizza comes Jo demonstrates how to prepare it: a capful of garlic sauce, then a thick squiggle of hot sauce. Folding a slice for a huge bite. Oil dripping into her cupped hand. Erik skeptical but eats three pieces. Scanning the pay-per-view movies, to Xie's relief no jokes about the porn options. They settle on *Terminator* and Erik sits in the chair, despite FKK's protest. There's room on the bed, Leni insists. I'm fine, he says. Karen at the very bottom, legs tucked, head on her arm. Xie in the middle. After the movie they play cards, Xie teaching the bastardized version of Rook he and his father invented. Leni yawning through the instructions. This is taking way too long. No, just pay attention, it's worth it once you get it. Karen playing impeccably. Taking trick after trick. Erik exclaiming, Goddamn it. Her wry grin. Leni making piles of cards according to her own rules. Jo snatching them up, elbowing Leni to the corner of the bed. Let the grown-ups play. Some discussion about what Jo's parents do, the business they own, water purification, Karen knowing someone who knows Jo's dad. What do you want to do when you graduate? she asks. Jo shrugs. What I'm doing. Work for the environment. Tipping her bottle of natural cola to her teeth. So no water filtration sales for you? Hell, no. Erik tilting back in the chair, arms crossed behind his head, biceps hard below the sleeve of his shirt. Jo opening a window to smoke and Karen takes a cigarette from her, elbow to elbow as they tap ash down on the concrete below. Hips out. Erik catching Xie's eye. Smiles. You almost ready for bed? Yeah. Gathering up the boxes and napkins. He had covered the body with branches, stones holding down the sheets, you just. Have to trust. That it exists and will go on existing. You get some rest, Erik says to the girls, and they nod. Night Mr. Lauridsen, night Xie, night Karen, night Jo, night Leni.

Long dream of the body, of that space between rib cage and spine, slightly electric when you enter it, feeling the bones from the inside; it always makes you come. Xie's mouth wet against the pillow, Erik snoring in the bed beside him. Not yet dawn beyond the curtains. Sore all over from the soft mattress, he hasn't slept so far from the floor in years. He rolls onto his back. Two hours before the alarm goes off. Imagine. The grid of the woods against the ceiling, your own dark head dead center. To make up for tonight, for the next night, you will do twice as many trees. Count them. Mark them now. You don't lose track, you keep them all right there, in your mind, in their thousands, the only math that matters. You don't even need the light from P. to see them. Your hands go from trunk to trunk without a single error. Even though they crack, splinter, groan, though it hurts them, you know how much stronger they will be. A drop of poison to hold back a sea. Bodies that can break blades, send the darkness running, cut the nightmare to pieces.

Xie takes granola and soy milk from the continental breakfast in the motel lobby. Leni looking longingly at a cherry Danish wrapped in plastic but Jo shakes her head: Devil, be gone. Jo's hair done up in extra-stiff spikes. That's a beautiful color, Karen says, admiring the deep green. Jo grins, elbowing Leni: This little chicken does all my dye jobs. Leni curtsies. Erik tucking their water bottles in a pack. They take a shuttle downtown, Xie's eyes fixed to the window, looking for their stop. Is that it? Erik says as they step off the shuttle, a thin trickle of people turning into a half-empty square. Jo puts her hand on his shoulder. It's that way. They go down two blocks, then turn around a corner and into a solid wall of bodies, an enormous crowd packing a boulevard headed by the capitol building. Karen exhales. Erik's hand hovers at Xie's back. Moving along the edges of the crowd Xie looks for E.A. shirts or stickers or patches but there are none. Prickle of uneasiness. I thought they organized this, he says. Jo looking straight ahead, little shake of her head, knowing something but it's too late to ask what. Xie bakes quietly in his hoodie, the unseasonably hot spring day made even hotter by the number of bodies trying to push closer to what they assume is a stage at the front steps of the city hall. Erik's jaw tight. Jo looking at her phone. So the speeches start at ten and then the march starts an hour after that. Lifting her head to scan for a place to sit or stand. A counterprotest crowd lines the sidewalks. COAL PUTS FOOD ON MY TABLE. WE SUPPORT JOBS FOR ALABAMA. SAVE A COAL MINER, KILL A TREE HUGGER. Leni snorts. Fucking CWA, she murmurs, and someone in the counterprotest catches her eye, as if hearing her, and she raises her middle finger. Erik gripping her wrist. Don't. Already something unpleasant in the dry air, restlessness in the crowd, people only half listening to the speech from Greenpeace, talking among themselves, looking at their phones. Shouts from the street to the sidewalk and back. Police watching from horses, from barricades separating the groups. Full riot gear. Vans with cameras mounted on their roofs. Erik wipes his face with his hand. We stay together, he says. I mean it. Mute nods. They sit on a wall outside the post office, listening to a speaker call out the names of species threatened by mining. Karen scribbling on a piece of paper. Are you taking *notes*? Jo laughs. Karen makes a face. Jo, hush. The list is so long it takes the speaker five minutes to get through it. Xie trying to ignore the shifting in his stomach. Another speaker smiles at the CWA crowd.

We don't want to take your jobs or disrespect your need to provide for your families. We want to protect the vibrancy of this beautiful state and turn attention away from short-term economic goals and toward sustainable, efficient, and healthy options for all energy workers in Alabama and beyond. CWA heckling her. No one buying it, not even the people on her side. The woman's smile so strained it looks as if it might break her wincing face by the time she's done. Erik, arms crossed, hip against the wall, scans the crowd, mouth set. Sweating through the back of his white T-shirt. Karen in jeans, sneakers, hair in a ponytail. First time he has seen her bare arms, freckled from shoulder to wrist. Still writing in her notebook. Someone says over the microphone, We are all here to celebrate the wondrous beauty of these precious mountains. Scattered applause. Someone calls out directions to turn and start the march; there's a mass shifting in the crowd but it doesn't go anywhere, people jammed up against each other's backs, increasingly airless. Why aren't we moving? Leni wonders, and Erik lifts her by the waist so she can see over the top of the group. Holy fucking shit, she whispers. A mass of black-masked, black-clothed figures slowly press against the momentum of the crowd, like a drop of blood unfurling in a glass of water. Many hundreds strong. One of the figures throws a bottle toward the sidewalk, hitting a CWA man in the face, busting his nose open. Like lighting a match. Everyone immediately yelling, shoving. Xie reaching for Jo's arm but there is more glass and then a sudden surge of bodies on both sides, some jumping the barriers, not enough police to maintain the line between the protesters and the CWA. Xie covers his head. A man reaching for Karen, blindly, why Karen of all people and she turns but there is nowhere to go, his hand is in her hair, brutal wrench of her head backward, her strangled yelp. Erik shouting, Hey, hey! Forcing his way between the man and Karen, Jo throwing a punch to someone's mouth, spray of blood and Leni's shriek and Xie a coward, eyes shut, body folded double. His father's arms around him, hard, holding him up, saying something to Jo and Jo not listening but Erik roars JO MOVE NOW, pushing them backward through the crowd just keep moving. Brutal brunt of bodies no air endless smash of glass smell of smoke and black masks filtering through the crowd, striking back at the police with clubs, pepper spray, bottles, elbows, knees, knives, vicious twist of bodies wanting to do the worst to other bodies. Thick adrenaline sweat and Jo and Erik plowing forward to a side street where runners rush past, through a toppled barricade, breaking off from the mass. Behind a Target they stop. Breathless. Erik's hands on Xie's shoulders, Are you okay? Karen murmuring to Leni, who holds her hand, finger swollen, trying not to cry, I'm fine. Jo red-faced, spitting into the gutter. Motherfuckers. Everyone just take a second, Erik says, panting. Just take a second. Still the sounds from the street. A siren. Looking over their shoulders to make sure no one coming toward them. Karen on her phone, calling a cab. Voice steady. Sniff. Leaning into the street to see the signs. Xie reaching to pull her back. Her arm out to ward him off. Yes. There's five of us. She hangs up. When their cab comes they squeeze in. Erik pure tension, Jo stroking Leni's hand. Xie's forehead against the glass. Karen rubbing the back of her skull. At the hotel Xie heads straight for bed, covers up, clothes on. Click of the door and Erik in the hall, with Jo. This is the second time, he says. The second time you've put my son in danger. What are you talking about, Jo says. Erik insisting: You said it would be peaceful. Of course I thought it would be, she says, but Erik stops her, voice rising just a step higher. Did you know that group would be there? What group? Jo, don't play dumb. The kids with the masks. Why do you assume they're all *kids*? Erik's voice rising. So you *did* know. Erik— Don't call me Erik. I'm not one of your friends, Jo. Jo's quick blink, Okay, Mr. Lauridsen. I anticipated some tension but I didn't know there would be a fucking *riot*, Jesus. But that's what you want, isn't it? Erik says. What do you mean? Look at your hand, Jo. You hit a man in the face. It took you a split second. So you tell me. Did you bring us all down here to watch you— Jo cutting him off, Hey, wait a second, I didn't ask you to come, I didn't ask *any*one to come, okay, it was Xie— Erik snorting, Am I wrong? Is there someone else in charge here? Jo raises her hands. I'm not responsible for what anyone else does. I'm sorry it got crazy but that's not what I intended and I certainly didn't *start* anything. Sometimes people get hurt and that's a risk we take. No, Erik says, it's a risk that *you* took, that *you* decided was acceptable. How irresponsible can you be? And Jo's frustrated inhale, chin trembling but she presses her lips together, hard, to stop it. We're fine, she insists. Erik shaking his head. No, no, we're not. Didn't you see how he just folded up out there? He can't protect himself, he won't. You don't know what he was like, before we came here, okay, you didn't see him lying in bed day after day, ready to cut his goddamn *throat* because of all this shit in his head, he just takes it in and he can't—he doesn't know what to do with it, and you want him to keep shoving his face in it, when it's—it's enough! Staring at Jo, who stares back. Deep breath. Look, whatever you're afraid of, whatever he's afraid of, it's already happening, okay? And he wants to *do* something about it. If there was some other option, some fantasyland where everything is going to be fine as long as we bury our heads in the sand, then believe me, I'd take it. But there's not. Not for me and not for Leni and not for Xie and if you think you can protect him by denying that then you're just—wrong. She holds Erik's gaze; after a moment he nods, the first to look away. Goes to Xie, sitting on the bed, his hand on Xie's flank. I'm going to order some food from the Mexican place. Xie nodding. Rice and beans and grilled vegetables in Styrofoam, he sits up to eat it. TV on. Erik on the bed beside him, gripping an enormous burrito. The protest on the news, a car on fire, a whole street of plate glass windows smashed, a line of ambulances beside a toppled barricade. Erik clicks past it. Xie eating only the vegetables, he can smell the chicken broth in the rice, the lard in the beans, but the onions are good, the peppers, cooked in fresh oil, salt, pepper, tender, he's trying. Everyone is trying. Remembering the call he made from the jail. Can you come pick me up. Whispering into the phone, he had inexplicably lost his voice. Two a.m. His father instantly awake, Where are you? And closing his eyes to say it, thumbing the silver slot on the pay phone: Downtown. At the jail. Erik said nothing, just got in his truck and drove. A horrible noise when he saw his son's face, streaked with blood, flesh darkening around his eye. Can you get him a goddamn bandage? Erik yelled, and a cop shuffled down the hall to show his contempt. Looks worse than it is, another cop said. You went up to that farm? Erik asked. You did what they said you did? Xie glanced at the cop. Then back at his dad. Nodded. Erik paid bail and cleaned his face and got him in the truck. They put them in cages, Xie said. Really small cages, and. I didn't hurt anyone. I just let them go. Erik looking at the road, fingers over his mouth, not trusting himself to say anything. Then, as now, his father slept in his bed, curled on top of the covers beside him. Xie doesn't brush his teeth, doesn't pee, just stays where he is. You don't feel anything. Just float to the ceiling. Stay there.

But in the morning he panics. Dreamed all night about. Screams and. No air. His father asleep and. Might die. I might die. He gets out of bed, heads for Karen's door, breathless knock. She opens in a second, brushing her teeth, green eyes sharp on his. Can I come in? Nod, steps aside, shutting the door with a quiet click. He sits on the edge of her unmade bed. Head in his hands. Trying to breathe. She moves quick to the sink, spits, wipes her mouth on the towel. Sits beside him. Hand on his back. Xie, just take a deep breath. But. Can't. Some sharp sense of death. Too close. Eating up all the air in his chest. Pain in his arms, hands, tingling to the tips of his fingers and his head. Eyes wide on his knees, which are shaking so bad, am I. Coming apart. Her head bent to his. Hair against his shoulder. It's just anxiety, Xie, you're okay. You're okay. Her bag on a chair. Bra and nightshirt and old underwear. Bottle on the nightstand, half full. Karen takes his hand, puts it beneath his T-shirt where. The medal is. He grips it, along with the cross. Eyes squeezed shut. Chest easing up, breath smoothing out. Karen looking at him. Okay? He swallows. Nods. Yeah. Sorry. Swallowing again. Drinking the water she offers, plastic cup from the bathroom, water like metal in his mouth. Don't worry about it, she says. A knock at the door; Erik there, looking from Karen to Xie, the unmade bed, Karen's bare legs. Good morning, Karen says. Xie needed some aspirin. I guess we're all a bit shaken up. Still. Erik's slow nod. Yeah. How is your head? he asks. Fine. Thanks. Going to her bag to get a bottle of Advil. Puts it in Xie's hand. There you go. Erik taking a step back. Hand on the door. Xie follows his father out. No breakfast. An hour later everyone in the car, quiet. Erik hands the iPod back to Jo and she scrolls through, puts on jazz. Leni sleeps against Jo's shoulder. Mouth open. Jo scratching the blue polish from her nails. Deer, horses, fields. Cracking the window for some air. They don't stop to eat, just drive straight through, and then they are home. As soon as they are inside Erik takes Xie's chin in his hand. Look at me. You okay? Xie pulling away. Dad. I really don't see the point of going down there, Erik says. Do you? Xie shrugs, exhausted again. I'm going to lie down. Erik calling out. Some people got hurt, Xie. It could have been one of us. Up the ladder. Layer of light over the entire floor. He walks on it. Pulls the branches from the body, clears away the stones. Slipping the sheet from the skull. A leaf ground to dust beneath his knee. Gather the body to his chest. P. swells into the room; the hammer on the floor. The light beyond the window. The birch aglow. Beloved. He puts the body down. Picks the hammer up.

E.A. was all over Alabama. Not just where he thought they would be, on the edges of the camp, contained, but more deeply embedded in the state than anyone could have guessed. The protesters in the city were only a distraction, planted to incite the exchange with the CWA and to set up the dummy camps clustered at the base of the mountains while the real center of the group, led by Alias, was hiking in from the north, from West Virginia and Kentucky, to converge at night in the foothills. Xie and FKK gather at Jo's to watch the video: a chain of protesters sitting cross-legged on the land marked by surveyor's flags, arm in arm, locked neck-to-neck. Everyone in black, no logos. The hair on Xie's arms standing up as the camera pans down the line, endless, he tries to count but loses track after a hundred, two hundred, the camera keeps marching on and still there is no limit.

A huge banner held up with poles driven into the dirt, white on black, WE WITNESS THE RAPE AND MURDER OF MOTHER NATURE. The line snakes up the foothills, protesters chained by the waist to trees, black bandannas covering their mouths, their heads. The video goes on for ten minutes, fifteen, no sound, and then suddenly cuts to Alias pinned by his shoulders to a tree, three men holding him there as the jaws of a bolt cutter clamp down on the lock around his waist, snapping the metal in half. Alias arching like a fish fighting for water, a constant hoarse bellow as a cop in riot gear rolls him over, knee in his back, Alias's cheek scraped deep on a stone, blood against the dirt. Xie touches his own face. Leni crying into the neck of her shirt. You can't take it, Alias screams, over and over. You can't take it. A boot hits him in the ribs once, twice. Fuck, Jo breathes, scrubbing her nose with the heel of her hand. The video cuts to a report about five million dollars' worth of clear-cutting equipment sabotaged in Guatemala, the E.A. sign painted in red on the side of a truck. A warrant for Nova's arrest, her face on camera, maskless. *Founder of an international terrorist organization.* Jo shuts the lid of her laptop. Xie's heart pounding. Leni curled on the bed. Did you know there would be so many of them? Xie asks. Jo still staring at the closed computer, mute shake of her head. I can't believe they're calling them terrorists, Leni says into the pillow. *They're* the fucking terrorists. Jo pushes the laptop beneath the bed, goes to the bathroom, shuts the door behind her. Xie just sits. He remembers what Nova said, about people like them always working in the dark;

and now Nova and Alias and all the rest there, in the light, the most dangerous place to be.

Guess that was our last field trip, Karen says, tired smirk. Both of them late to the library, meeting on the steps to walk in together, ignoring Greg's stare. Yeah. Sorry it didn't turn out how—how I thought it would. If I'd known— She shrugs, dropping into her chair, brushing bits of eraser from the table with her arm. Wasn't your fault. Things happen. My mom saw us on the news, he says. Us? Really? Yeah. She screamed at my dad for like an hour. Karen groans. Poor Erik. Are they still arresting people? He nods. Yeah. He looks out the window. Quiet. Karen crossing her wrists on the table, click of her small watch against the wood. I finished *Interior Castle*, she says. He makes a face. I don't know why I asked you to read it. I was happy to, Karen says. I thought you liked it. You marked almost every page. I know, I did like it. But. I think I got it wrong. How so? Xie twisting his lip between his fingers. The whole thing is just about being in love with God and that's all she talks about, like, it's not even about being a Christian, you know, *doing* things, I mean at least Jesus wanted to help people but she just thought. Like. Praying was the best thing you could do. Like that was going to change anything. She was a nun, Xie, the book was written for other nuns, cloistered nuns, not people like you and me. Their job was pretty much to do exactly what she's writing about. But, so? Why should anyone be a nun? The words more bitter than he means. Karen spreads her fingers on the table. I think she *was* trying to help people. She wanted them to experience the pleasure, the joy she thought was possible. Don't you think that's generous? Or good? Xie shakes his head. It just seems. Like a waste. Wait, being in love is a waste? If you think that's the most important thing, like, that that's the point of being alive, then . . . yeah. She thought the world was evil but she didn't do anything to change it, it's like she thought the best thing to do was just wait to die so she could be in heaven and everything would be perfect for her and fuck everything else, you know? Come on, Xie, that's not what she was saying. The book is called *Interior Castle*, it's about what's going on inside a person, that's the whole point. She wasn't writing a political manifesto. Yeah, well, maybe she should have. Karen shrugs. Maybe you're right. But I think you're being a little too hard on her. Quiet. In the corner of the library a little boy karate-chops a stack of foam blocks. Do you think she was crazy, Xie says. I mean, that's what she was, right? Karen blinks. How do you mean. Like if I said. The things that she said, then. You would think I was crazy. Right? Does it matter if she was? Karen asks. Of course it does. Why? Because then it's not true, he says. What's not true? Everything. Look, Karen says, if she was insane, then so are all religious people. So is everyone who believes in something that most other people don't, whether you can prove it or not. Facts don't convince people. Faith does. Xie scoffs. You think that's a good thing? No, she says, sighing. But it's a thing. Quiet. I saw something once, Xie says. Leaning over the table. Hair in his face. Karen goes very still. He presses the eraser of his pencil into his forehead, closes his eyes. I keep seeing it. Her hand on his hand. What is wrong with you, he thinks. That you want only bones, how are you any better than Teresa, than all the ones like her, saints, martyrs, mystics, people who fought only for the right to forget the world, to forget the flesh. And yet. The body belongs to the earth. It is the earth itself. He opens his eyes. The sun pouring in through the windows, hot yellow squares on the carpet, on his back. Let's just do the stupid algebra, he says, and Karen stays close for a moment, leaning over the desk. Fuck algebra, she says, looking him in the eye. Xie chuffs. If you want to fuck algebra we'll fuck algebra, he says, and she laughs, loud, head back, there is gold in the air when she does it, not coming from P. but from her, and he almost says, Look.

Jo at graduation. They all go. Even Erik. Sit in the stands with Leni, Jo's parents on their left, curt hellos. It will never stop being a surprise. How much people dislike you. Sit there and don't look at anyone. Let your father brush the hood back from your face. Smile so wide when you see Jo in her blue cap and gown, her hair brushed straight back over her head, clean, shiny. You don't believe in any of it but. Believe in her. Clap. Whistle. Leni screaming, WE LOVE YOU, JO! Jo dropping a heavy curtsy, shaking the principal's hand, 4.2 GPA. Leni always said she didn't even have to try. But she tries at everything. Proving something. That she can be what she wants, an outcast and a nerd and a rich kid and an anarchist and a credit to her school and a threat to her nation. James Moore's shoulder next to hers as they stand for a class photo. Turning afterward to shake her hand. The sun so strong. Erik kissing her cheek. Proud of you. She smiles. Why, thank you, Mr. Lauridsen. I'm proud of you, too. Flinging her cap in the trash, ruffling her hair, Fuck, let's get *out* of here.

Dark club to celebrate. Forty-five minutes in the car, some crazy music blasting. Xie yelling, What is this? What? What is this! he screams again. The Knife! Leni yells in his ear, fishnet top and tiny black bra, concave thighs in a skirt cut from something longer, frayed uneven edge against her bare skin. You didn't dress up, she complained when she saw him but Xie smiled, coy, Yes, I did, and she shrieked, seeing the eyeliner traced along his lashes. Jo's hair spiked so high it rivals even P.'s helmet in its glory. Smoking in the car with the windows up, Xie recalling the time in Jo's room, crawling along the carpet, a lifetime ago. Doesn't put his mouth on the joint when it is passed his way but holds it for Leni, her lips barely touching his fingers. Roads and roads and roads. Avoiding the interstate. At the edge of the university town an abandoned building. Unlit street. Code word and no IDs, Leni looking over her shoulder at Xie with a grin. Inside a room the size of the library, concrete pillars painted black and graffiti everywhere. Blue light and so hot, a DJ in the corner and kegs of beer, a shelf nailed to one long wall to serve as a bar, stacked with plastic cups. Jugs of water. Stenciled on the wall: STAY SAFE. Absolute crush of bodies. Sea of heads. Like a protest but better. Jo and Leni get beers and he drinks water. Refusing the new joint Jo lights. Leni cutting right into the dance floor after her first drink, arms up, rhythmless. Jo's last deep inhale, brow furrowed, smoke packed at the back of her throat. You want to dance? Yeah, in a minute, I. Just have to. Get used to it. After a long critical look Jo says, You have a thing. About crowds. He snorts. News flash. All right, but you are fucking dancing tonight, so. Drink your water and meditate or whatever you have to do before I drag your ass out here. Xie nods. Yes, sir. Jo going after Leni, folding into the mass of flesh. Nice that for a while no one is noticing him or expecting anything of him, he can just. Stand here. Do nothing. All these young people. Not angry or sad or making plans or. Anything. Just get out of your head. And even against the wall it feels good. To be here. Lose track of time. Eventually Leni iridescent with sweat struggling through the crowd to put her hand on his wrist. Come on. No patience for the split second of his hesitation: If you don't drink and won't smoke and won't dance you're not going to enjoy yourself. He shrugs. I'm enjoying myself. She wipes her forehead on her arm. Come *on*. Her hands on his wrists. Jo coming over, What did I tell you about this fucking hoodie, Xie? Grabbing the bottom and yanking it over his head. Oh my god, I don't think I've ever seen your *arms*. Gripping his biceps. All of them grinning. Jo flipping up the end of his black T-shirt and whistling, Oh, but baby doll's almost got a six-pack! And high-fiving him, his hoodie balled on the counter along with the beers, a song from the album in the car repeating in the club and this time he goes with them, pushing to the center of the dance floor, he doesn't know what to do but everyone seems to be more or less jumping so they, too, are jumping, in time to the blue strobes, all these bodies around him, screaming the chorus. Sweat and sticky floor and smell of yeast. His arms flailing, Leni's hair hitting his shoulder. Jo's lateral thrash, cleavage to her chin, and he laughs, breathless, why did he never even imagine. Dancing. And P. there, every time the strobe flashes on, moving through the crowd, until. Behind Xie. If only he could lean. Back into him, be held, for once, among others, be held so others could see. Song bleeding into song. Jo and Leni with their arms around his neck, the three of them in a huddle, heads bent to center where P. stands, gold glow against the blue. Panting through their smiles. He can't feel his legs they just. Keep moving. A Cure song comes on and he sings with everyone else. Dumb off-key voice. Sweat stinging his eyes. No way to move without touching someone but somehow it's. Okay. No one here afraid of being hurt by the other bodies. No one afraid of being caught even though everything about this place is illegal. Leni grinning, her face seized with joy. Xie's hair sticking to his face, his neck, a burn licking his lungs. Coming down so hard, again and again, on the concrete floor.

They break to pee. Jo fanning her face with her shirt, Xie's own shirt gone, the girls pulled it off somewhere on the dance floor and he is as naked as he's been in public for a long time. Flushed but a sudden chill, skin prickling. Do you see me, beloved. Jo off talking in a corner, shoulder against the wall, hands moving, almost forehead-to-forehead with another girl, tall, mess of curly hair, bucktoothed, has he seen her before? Leni and Xie sit against the narrow bar, Leni's feet hooked on the rungs of a stool, knees tight together, cupping her elbows. Xie's back slick against the gritty concrete. Leni pulling the medal from his chest, finger hooked around the chain. What's this? Having to shout. Um. That's my patron saint. Leni frowning. What? Peering at the image. He was a, uh. Kid who. Died because he wouldn't convert to paganism. But you're a pagan, Leni says, smiling, rubbing her thumb over the medal. He moves his hair from his eyes. I am? Yeah, you're always like. In the woods and worshipping the earth and stuff. He smiles. Yeah, I guess. Why do you wear it? Xie shrugs. Catholics wear them for. Protection or. Like, help. Leni nodding, quick glance to see if he is serious, then she is serious, too. Letting the necklace go. It's really pretty. Looking over her shoulder to see Jo laughing, her laugh carries all the way through the room. P. dancing alone in the center of the crowd. Peter found a new space, Leni says. They let him rent at a different church, it's nice. You should come sometime. It's all the same people. And some new ones, Jo's been spreading the word. Xie snorts. Looks like she's got a fresh one now. Leni's wry smile. Yeah. She's good at it. Finding people, you know? Like, I never would have talked to you, at school. I was kind of worried, when she said we should. Why? She tugs a piece of her hair, head cocked. I wanted her to myself, I guess. Or I just didn't know if things would be as good with another person. She smiles. But she was right. You were one of us. Her eyes scan his, deep gray. What do they want to see? He tries not to look away. She puts her hand in his, fingers against the calluses. Let's go dance, she says. And they do.

They are in the middle of the woods. Half the trees spiked, half to go, his pace has been perfect but there are still so many to do, and the worry that he will not be done in time, that he will miss one of them, the wrong one, the one that will be cut first, never goes away. When he finally falls asleep at night he is hammering, when he is fucking the body he is hammering, when he is reading he is hammering, hands so hard now, a layer of skin as tough as wood. The canvas of his sneakers worn completely through at both sides, hoodie filthy, he washes it while standing in the shower fully dressed, the water black between his feet. Now stumbling in the ferns, shin skinned on the raw edge of a log, the new leaves on the youngest trees lashing his eyes. Rash of tick bites on his spine. The endless ring of the hammer hitting the nail, he hears it in his sleep, second pulse in his brain, who else. Understands this sound. It cuts through the night. And now P. lying down in the dirt, Xie looking over his shoulder to see, What are you doing. Rest, beloved. Are you fucking kidding? Pulling the next nail from his pack, two more between his teeth. Press the tip against the tree, chest-high; if he drove it through his own chest, at this angle, the nail would graze the top of his twelfth vertebra. Deep breath. Holds it. The nail falling through the birch. The next nail where his pelvis would be; the last at the ankles. Even if the tree was cut at the base, somehow missing the first nail, the others would stop the machines in a mill, making the tree impossible to process. He clips the heads of the nails, collects the metal in his pocket. Moves to the next tree. Adjusting the pack to the opposite shoulder but fumbles, dropping it, nails splashing through the ferns, Goddamn it. Kneeling to push them back into the pack. While he's there, make the *X* at the roots, quick hard cut, P. turning onto his silver stomach: if they are meant to be destroyed they will be destroyed, he says. Xie incredulous. If we don't finish this, then yeah, they will be. Next tree. Are you saying it doesn't matter either way? How does that make sense? P. quiet. I should just, what, go to bed while someone comes in here and chops it all down? Three more nails. I mean, what is your point. You carry a sword but you don't even use it. What, beloved, do you want to use it? P. asks. Jesus fucking Christ! Xie shouts. Just get up and help me! P.'s hand suddenly around Xie's wrist, squeezing. Xie yanks his arm away, sending the back of his own wrist straight into a trunk, hard, and without thinking he turns and strikes the birch with the hammer, shouting, so much anger left in that aching shoulder, enough to break through the bark, show the deep gold beneath. Startle of birds against the clouds. Xie panting, dropping the hammer, both palms immediately against the tree. Forehead to the back of your hands. Why did you call me here, Xie asks. What do you want me to do. P.'s hands on his hips from behind. That breath that is not breath on his neck. Night heavy on his head. I didn't call you, beloved. You called yourself.

There is only one more meeting at the library before summer. Karen at their table, filling out a form. Her hair cut to the chin. I like it, he says. Looks rad. She smiles. Touches the shorn ends. Thanks. Deep breath. So. Almost free, yeah? She pushes a packet of papers in his direction. He flips through them—forms to fill out, things to sign, he won't do any of it, but. Folds them into his bag anyway. Putting a couple of jars of jam on the table. I got Greg something. She laughs. Nice. He'll love it. Yeah, I hope so. I made some for you, too. She takes the jar, thumbing the label, on which he has drawn a star. Why'd you cut your hair? Oh, she says. A change. Are you growing yours out? He palms his hair back; his bangs to his cheekbones now, the rest falling over his collar. I'm just lazy, he says. Glancing around the room, hopefully for the last time: the yellow wood glowless on the tables, construction paper flowers stuck to the windows, the formerly flourescent sun bleached near-white. What do you see yourself doing? Karen asks. After high school? P. bright in the corner of his eye. Remember. How it was. When you first brought him home. And how even this place, for a little while, was radiant. I just want to find a way to live, he says. Karen nods, looking at her hands. Me, too. A breath. Well, she says. Tell the girls hello from me. Maybe we can do something this summer. Get tea or lunch some-where. Sure, he says. They pack their things. Get up to go. And, Xie? He turns. Yeah? Her eyes scanning his. Maybe you can tell me about your friend sometime. Xie not knowing what to say to that. So he just goes.

MacAdams calls, meets with his father. He has failed his junior year, but can attend classes at the school if he agrees to the following, etc., etc. Erik saying, You can write them a letter telling them you aren't going back. Getting up from the table for more soup. Just let me know what you decide. It's an effort to take a breath, to nod, to say, Yeah, I will. As if he is considering something when everything has been considered already, decided already. His father lifting the spoon to his mouth. The soup is delicious; he has become a good cook, in spite of himself. What have you been doing in the garden? Erik asks. What about the garden. Erik cocking his head. The sunflowers. They're almost as tall as the roof.

In the mail, a heavy package for him: a pair of bolt cut-ters, the ones he'd had at the Moore farm, seized by the police and now here, months later. They belong to Leni, who never said where she got them; brand-new, beautiful, shiny red handles, black blades at the head; he remembers the heft of them, how they felt in his hands, made to destroy the things meant to keep you out. He looks up Leni's address in the phone book, the name of a street miles from his house, from Jo's, from school, he has to look at a map to find it. Astonished when he arrives. The wheels of his bicycle sliding on the wet dirt road: no sidewalk, just this mud creeping up to the door of a house that looks as if it is sinking into the ground, tarpaper on the roof, sun-bleached plastic and car parts littering the yard bounded by a half-collapsed fence. A little girl in a diaper squats at the corner of the house and puts her hand up the spout of a bent drainpipe, singing. Her eyes slit at Xie. Hey, he says. Leni! the girl shouts, thin-voiced. A moment later Leni leaping out across the mud, frantic. What's wrong? Where's Jo? Nothing's wrong, he says. Leni scratching her arm, baggy plaid shirt and blue jeans, pale face, hunted eyes unlined, no ring in her nose, like a child dressed in her brother's clothes. I just—got these, and I—wanted to bring them to you. Get inside, Leni barks to the girl, but the girl continues singing, paying no attention. He gives Leni the cutters and she takes them, quick, long unbuttoned cuff flapping around her wrist. You can't just—come here, she says. I'm sorry, I— haven't seen you guys in a while and I thought—I'd bring them, he stammers. There's a thing called a phone, she says. I'm sorry, he repeats. They stand there. Where have you been? she asks. Just—home, he says. Leni looks over her shoulder at the house, then back at him. Holding the cutters out. I don't need these, she says, and he takes them. I have to go. She walks back to the house, taking the girl by the arm, careful not to slam the screen door hanging from one hinge as they go inside. Dark sheets in all the windows. He thinks of the sounds the mink made in their cages, that restless rustle of fur. There is no sound at all from inside Leni's house. A fat drop of rain hits the back of his hand. What do you do with all the living things in trouble. Build a church. Build a bomb. He pulls his hood up, turns his bike in the mud. When he looks over his shoulder the little girl is peeking through a hole in the screen. He waves. She waves back.

Walk through the park downtown on the way home from the garden store, cucumber seeds in his pocket. Brown grass, broken swings, sagging chain-link softball cages; why be here when you could be. Anywhere in the woods. A slim column of smoke twists up from the barbecue pits on the other side of the cinder-block restrooms; voices, laughter. A chill. Have to go around to get to the fountain. Shot of dread in your chest when you see: Ryan Moore and a dozen others at one of the pits. You know they see you. Shaking as you bend your head to the fountain. Throat too tight to swallow, you let the water run out of your mouth. Frozen there for a moment. Clink of P. somewhere. If someone tried to hurt you would he. Just watch or. Hey, Moore calls. That you, Twilight? Xie straightens, wiping water from his chin. Thirsty? You want a burger to wash that down with? Laughter. We got some fresh baby deer right here. Patting the side of a red cooler. Better than tofu. Don't even glance at them. Head down. Keep walking. But Moore's wife, he doesn't know her name, jogging up to Xie, puts her arm through his. Hey, wait a sec. It's Xie, right? Her shoulder banging into his. Come have a beer. Smiling. Big silver hoops in her ears, hair in braids. Come on. Pulling on his arm. If he pulled back she'd trip, her boots have some kind of crazy high heels on them, she can barely walk. Come on, please? she says, tipping her head. We won't bite. Promise. Gray eyes half kind. Lets her turn him around. Moore opens a can of beer, hands it to him. Dark eyes intent on his. Hollow cheeks, weak chin. Cheers, Twilight. Xie blinks. The woman, her name is Cherry, keeps her hand on his arm. Passes him a can of Pringles. You can eat these, right? Chips? A potato's a vegetable, yeah? Not knowing what to do. He bites one in half and it shatters in his mouth. Holds the beer without drinking it. P. behind the grill, smoke in his eyes. Becoming his eyes. Take a seat, Moore says, and a hole opens up in the group, making room. So how old are you? Cherry asks, sitting down beside him on a plastic crate. Sixteen, Xie mumbles. Cool. You driving yet? Head hunched low between his shoulders. No. Really? Shit, when I was your age I couldn't wait to drive. I was seventeen when I got my first truck. You see that blue one over there? That's my baby. He glances. Spotless chrome. Enormous wheels. Nice, he whispers. She drinks, arm still through Xie's. Aware that everyone is watching. Cherry with her small talk holding them off. Drink up, she says. You don't want that to go flat. He sips the beer. Try not to make a face. The sky as gray as a dirty glove. Facing the grill, just a few feet away, the lid of the cooler open to show its slick cargo. Full to the brim. Ryan's back to him, tall and broad in blue plaid, Gotta get some meat on your bones, son. Those beans ain't treating you right. Cherry smiles into her beer. Blood spits on the coals. Xie pulls the collar of his shirt over his nose. Moore lifts a brow. You know mink are cannibals, right? Some of the ones you let go ate the fuck out of each other. Mean little bastards. We treat them a hell of a lot nicer than they treat anything. Fresh water, all the meat they can eat. Moore throwing steaks over the flames. Sniff. We got some new ones, nice silver babies. Breeding real well. Taste like shit, though. No fat on 'em. Without looking Ryan passes a metal spatula to Xie. You turn these for me, will you? When Xie doesn't move one of the guys pushes his shoulder. Not too hard. Come on. It's fresh. Totally organic. Isn't that what you're all about, Twilight? Farm-to-table? Nudging his hand with the spatula. P. terrible in the smoke, looming over them all. Xie steps forward. Don't think, just. Pull the meat straight from the grill. Burning on one side, still wet on the other, red all the way through. Throwing it into the dirt. You fucking murderers! he shouts. Ryan's arm around his neck in a second, cutting off the last word. Right in his ear, like before, Listen I don't want to hurt you but you're asking for it, you crazy fuck. Cherry with her hand on Moore's back. Ry, don't, come on. And Moore turning his head, sharp. Calm down, I'm not gonna do nothing. Xie struggling with all his strength but Moore's embrace is like iron, there is nowhere for Xie to put his anger, sneakers digging into the ground. We invite you to hang with us and all you can do is act like a goddamn psycho, Moore hisses. What did we ever do to you, huh? You can't let people live their lives? You don't know shit about me, you little fuck. Suddenly letting him go. Spits in the dirt. Xie stumbles, gasping for air. Cherry squatting in those fucked-up shoes, tossing the steak to the dogs. Refusing to look at him. If Moore said the word they would be on him in a second. But he let Xie go and Xie goes. Turning his back. P. right behind him, those footsteps. Guardian. But too late. P.'s hand on his arm. Xie shrinking from it, accusing, You didn't do anything. You never do anything. Xie forgetting himself, speaking out loud. How often do I do that. Talk and not know I am talking. Walking too fast, tripping, fury throwing him forward. Clutching his own head as if to. Break it. The sole of his sneaker unglued, gaping at the sides with every step. What do you want me to do, beloved. Stop them! Stop— something! Even you can see how fucked-up it is, how *proud* they are of it. Past the church. Sounds of Mass. Body of Christ. Bringing his feet down harder and harder, as if to strike right through the earth. Through the skin of weeds into the woods. What does it matter, P. says. Leave them. Leave them what? Leave them *alone*? They just—they keep buying *more*, with *our* money, they think I'm going to laugh with them about. About frying animals on a fucking fire. Starting to sob, loud, helpless, They gas them, did you know that, they pack them into that barn, like fucking Nazis, and I'm the one who's wrong? I'm the fucking psycho? Fuck it, I'm going back, I don't care what happens, I'm going to blow their god-damn *house* the fuck *up*— and P.'s arm, from behind, around his neck, silver smooth across his throat, press-

ing. Down. Heart jumping against his ribs. Then shoved,
hard, full sprawl into the ferns, his chin hitting a stone,
hard click of teeth, the breath knocked free of his chest.
Dull shock. Slow press of palms in the dirt and even
slower to rise. In the trees now the tip of P.'s finger against
his forehead. Xie moves his head but the finger follows.
Insistent. Stop, Xie says. But P. won't. Pushing so that the
back of Xie's head is pinned to a birch. Piercing the skin.
Line of blood down his nose. Terror. Pure, crystalline.
You don't know what he can do. Imagines the finger
touching through to his skull, bone to bone. Pain sparkling between his eyes. Blood in Xie's mouth. Rubs it
from his lips, to look; there it is, bright on the back of his
hand. But no wound, the flesh on his forehead intact.
Remember. Hitting the tree with the hammer. The cracks
in the skin of the birch. Quick adrenaline pant, What is
this. This is you. This is the violence inside you. But you're
the one who showed me. You were there in the woods.
You put the nails in my hands. Yes, but not so you could
raise it against them. Against who? Your fellows. They
aren't my fucking *fellows*! Xie turning his head, trying to
stop crying. I don't even know what you are. Thinking, P.
didn't spare the lamb because he loved it, but because he
loved nothing. On earth. But you love the lamb, not as a
god, not as a symbol, but as itself, why isn't that enough?
No one has the right. To make a life into a sign. P.'s hand
on his chest, pressing. Xie pushes it away. As hard as he
can. No. He says it aloud, again: No. The light flickers, or
is it P., is he flickering, and what does it mean, the light
flinching like that, like something. Snapped. Can you

hurt him. Can you hurt something that is dead. Closes his eyes. I don't want to see it leaving, if it leaves. It does. It vanishes completely. You told it to go and it went. He opens his eyes. And it is darker here, much darker, than it has ever been before.

He can hammer with both his left and his right hand; he can hit the nail with his eyes closed, can drive it to the head with a single blow. The trees gave him a new body, one devoted to them, a servant to the hard flesh of the birch. Don't think. About P. You can do it alone; he showed you how. Erik is gone another night; you take the body from the attic, you lay it in the ferns. You cry without knowing you are crying. How uncanny that skull is, P. but not P., it cannot speak to you, cannot see what you have done, and now you feel such disgust, exposing it, exposing yourself, for what? Because you are lonely? Sad? Insane? The body is just as at home in your arms as it is in the dirt, it has no way of knowing. What you are doing or why. What is coming. How stupid to think you could live the way it does, gently, at rest; you are still flesh and the demands of the flesh are immense, not content with vegetables in a basket or flowers on a vine but an entire cathedral of being, which is what P. was, purely, directed at you, for you, the way nature never is, selfish to want it still but how to stop? In the woods with P. you were a god. Now you are just a boy. You take the body back to the attic. Put its hands on your face. You cannot say it, because it's not your word: beloved.

You are at the last line of trees. The deer no longer mind the noise; they watch it happen, the moment when the final nail sinks into the final trunk. All the woods at your back, a deep presence, alert, wondering if you are done doing your damage. You thumb the dark eyes in the bark, the headless tips of the nails. Look at you. Beauty. The leaves twitching on their stems, faint breeze. They are exhausted, too. From wondering. What it means. He rests his forehead against the trunk. Drops the hammer in the dirt.

They get a notice about the noise the saws will make while taking down the trees. Erik rubbing his thumbnail over his lower lip as he reads. What is it, Xie says. Silent push of the paper across the table. The woods are private property and should not be walked through or picnicked in or otherwise trespassed. No one can be liable for accidents involving logging equipment during such-and-such hours on such-and-such days. Any questions please call. Erik watching his face. Xie, he says. Caressing his wrist. Xie staring at the letter. Slow bloom of blood in his face. Erik leans forward, tightening his grip. Xie, he says again. Maybe there's someone we can talk to, the city council, get some of your friends involved, maybe Jo knows— Xie looks up. Furious smile. He pushes the paper away, stands. Goes to the kitchen. Turns the oven on, whisper of flame rushing from the jet. He breaks a head of cauliflower into creamy white pieces. A hundred branches beneath his knife. Erik follows. Leaning in the doorway. We don't know how bad it will be. The notice is only for one week of work. Xie nods. Dumping the cauliflower in the pot. Could be they only take a few hundred, at most. Xie still nodding, opening a can of chickpeas. Bangs it on the side of the pot to loosen the beans stuck to the bottom. It's okay to be worried about it. I know how you feel about those woods. Erik goes on, offering to write a letter, to meet with the property owners, maybe they could even buy some of the land, take out a loan, he'd been thinking of it for a while, a handful of acres maybe, maybe, maybe. Xie slapping each vegetable on the board. Kale, a sweet potato, tomatoes. It was P. who sharpened the knife last, it cuts. Beautifully. We're having curry tonight, Xie interrupts. That all right with you? Erik stops. Xie continuing in silence, lowering the flame on the rice. Wiping his hand on the towel. I'm not worried about it, Xie says, okay? Speaking into the sink. Gripping the lip of the stainless steel. So it's fine. Erik's face in the window, trying to catch Xie's eye in the glass.

There are no more spikes left in the boxes. He breaks down the cardboard, buries the hammer in the garden. The gloves. His pack. Dirt warm in his hands. While you're here strip the beds of old lettuce and put in new seeds. The cucumbers against the fence. There are tomatoes everywhere, and melons as heavy as heads. Worms churning in the compost. The strawberries ready for fresh jam. He'll put it all in a box tomorrow, for Peter, bike it to the new church. But what to do now. Look across the stream. Moonlight running down every trunk, hash marks in the dark, white black white black white. What did I miss, what did I do wrong. But there is nothing wrong. Each tree in its place, fully crowned in green.

He goes into the little box, sits. He is supposed to say something. The latticed grille, through which he can see only a shadow, exudes a smell of rosewater. His breathing so loud. Yes? prompts the priest. Xie swallows. Tongue stuck. How long has it been since your last confession. He rubs his face. When has he ever told anyone anything? Really told them. Long silence. The priest waits. What do people say, here? Sins only the church can address. The priest can't forgive someone for gassing a farm full of mink. Or eating a steak. Or cutting down a tree. He can't forgive what isn't a sin. He doesn't even know what sin is. In Teresa's mansions there are no animals, no plants, nothing living at all; those are left outside the castle, in the dirt, along with the most tortured souls, and the farther you get from them the better you are, cleaner; is that what they all believe, what this priest believes, what he teaches, that nature is garbage, is evil, and only when you free yourself of all that is living do you reach what is good. You piece of shit, Xie whispers. The priest is silent. Xie pushes out, the door squealing on its brass hinge. The church like the house, his attic, safe only if you are content to live like a fucking fool. His father can't understand it, why he can't be completely happy even in the garden, in the woods, when he is free to do as he pleases, to make the sort of life he wants, Erik allowing him every possible freedom, not understanding that the only available context for that freedom is poison. A comfortable existence borrowed against total collapse. *Do what arouses you to love,* Teresa wrote, again and again: never what arouses you to anger, to rage. It's no spirit that loves the woods; only a body is capable of it, one that keeps its eyes on the ground, in the meat of the earth. And yet it is also the flesh that blinds you. Cripples you. Because what you came here to say is: What do I have to do to have him back. Can you bring him back to me. Looking for him everywhere. The red glass in the windows, liquid in the sun. The dandelions clustered against the stone, the tallest things growing on the denuded land, land cleared so that the church could sit in silence on the dirt, facing the woods, friend or foe? It is the only place left that could hold on to the body, that kept it for you. You can't untangle one from another. Do you have to? Anything less than union is hell. Such a sharp line, between the field and the trees. You cross it for the last time.

He goes to the Moore farm. Same road, same time of night. Hasn't been. Since. Familiar but in a strange way, like something in a movie coming to life, the sagging porches, the abandoned Waffle House, all the dense oak and ash and in between the shadow of the mountains. Stands at the edge of the driveway. Little red eye of the camera in the tree. It's okay. You can see me. I can see you. No mask this time. He doesn't go past the house, stays in the mouth of the drive. Can hear them from here. Rustle. Rattle. Fur against fur, fur against steel. New babies in the nesting boxes. What's it like. Never to belong to yourself. Maybe we all know. That's why we kill ourselves. Poison the world you can't have, that doesn't want you, that knows. What a virus you are. On the face of the earth. Moore's white truck a ghost in the night, glowing. He can still feel the teeth through the glove, the claws, if you free them then they are free to kill. Free to die another kind of death. A light switching on over the porch. Moore's face in the window. Calm. They look at each other. Wind stroking Xie's face. Here you can still see the stars. Not like in the city. They don't care about what happens. They go on burning whether or not you know their names, arrange them into shapes, make them into a story. If you look at the sky you see how much coldness there is in the way everything was created. But if you dig, the dirt is always warm. A burning at the heart of the earth. And everything stuck somewhere in between the deep freeze and the fire. Moore holding down a slat in the blinds. Unpanicked. He was never your absolute enemy; he, too, is merely living, the way he knows how. But when the trees are safe and your father is no longer responsible for what you do you will come back, here, to do more than just look. Moore in the yellow frame of the window. Touching two fingers to his brow in a salute.

The letter did not give a time; the truck could come today, or today, or today. There is nothing to do but wait. The body in his arms, in bed, for the first time without pleasure. Look into the eyes, which can never again

look back. It is not you. Not yet. Play cards with your
dad. Watch the news. Make dinner. Jo calls, Peter calls;
you don't answer. Knee never stops trembling. Won't he
come? Now that you've done it, shouldn't he see. The
woods as you both have made them?

Off the road the first two hundred trees are marked with
orange plastic tied around their trunks. Ends snapping
in the breeze. He strokes the warm, slick ribbons. Tries to
tear off a piece; the plastic stretches, whitens, but remains.
He lets it go. How hot the day is. Dry. His lips burning.
Blackbirds jumping from branch to branch. There are
tracks in the dirt, from where the men dragged their
boots, the door of their truck ajar on the road. Glint of
silver inside, all the teeth of the saw. Don't cry. Jo sobbing
in the hall. Erik alone by the lake. Karen in the car. Leni
shutting the broken screen. The tides turning red on one
coast, black on the other. Alias's mountains slashed to the
quick. P. pinning him against the trunk of the tree. Hip-
to-hip. What was the name of the lamb? It never had one.

You are asleep when the sound of the saw starts and then
you are awake.

The first cut. The first tree. Whine of something wrong
in a machine and then. No time to scream. No one
would expect spikes here, the birch part of no great

forest or preserve or endangered species, housing no extraordinary creatures, just common trees on private land. So no special mask or saw, no anticipation of anything. Wrong. Just a man doing a favor for a friend. Bending at the base of the birch. Say your prayers. The blade strikes the nail and the saw shatters, a piece of its chain sharper and faster than a sword in a hand spinning straight to the neck. Cutting one thing clean away from another. A body falling to the ground. A body falling in two parts.

Does a light come through the window, strike him on the forehead, call him to the half-cut tree. Or is it an absence of light that draws him. Life goes. Somewhere. When it goes. The man in the forest hanging just above or below his body for a moment, watching his own eyes wash red. Or is he evaporating along with his flesh. Forgetting he ever existed. You can imagine any number of things happening in this fragile pool of time. Silence where there should be sound. The birch cut half through at the base, brutal gape. Sap sorting itself around the wound. The soil drunk on blood. A body in a shape it was not meant to make. The sun pure and hard on the yellow plastic of the saw, the steel of its split chain. Xie steps backward, slow, until his heel hits the fender of the truck. Ragged sip of air. Hand against the hood, still warm. Every day before this one suddenly halcyon. It was so good. Not to see death coming.

———————

There are woods beyond the birch, you know them, you will get to know them, you can. Disappear. No one will know for hours, yet, about the body by the truck, about you, what you are. You don't think the word. The one that means: he who brings death. Mist of blood in the air. Over the dirt. Snap through the branches, the leaves, hands scraped raw, opening the old wounds. Air hard through the lungs, you can run and run and run. An animal from its cage, blind hurtle into the road. You keep the church to your left, you won't go near it, you are headed for the highway, beyond which stand the ash and the gum trees, clustered at the base of the mountains. Don't think of Erik. Of Karen. Of Leni. Of Jo. Peter's sad eyes. Nova's scars. The body you left behind. All your marks on the trunks. X after X after X. You run too fast to see them. The birch a white blur on either side, in front, behind, a sea, a sea of silver, then suddenly. Of gold. You stop. Are stopped. Hand out to touch the tree, which is no tree, but the body of the other. Enormous. Beloved. Only the sound of your breathing, of your blood. A crow twitching on its branch. Help me. P. pulling you down among the ferns. Shin on a stone. All you had to do was come here. To find him. If he was silent it was because you were silent; if he was far it was because you were far. But you were afraid. Still. Your face split by sobs, I didn't know, I didn't know. That the body in the woods would open up that way, irreversibly, you had not imagined what could happen to it, to you, how it might split you from life to take life. Fingers sunk into the dirt. Your head on his boot. Let me disappear. And his hand on your chin, pulling your head up to look at him, those eyes, black pools, Listen. There is no other world into which you might vanish. You must stay on the road. You must get on your knees. You must wait for the sword.

The perimeter of the woods is bound in yellow tape. Inside, it is busy with flesh; they want to know. If there is a mark on every tree. Hand after hand over trunk after trunk, scouting out the scars. And they are astonished, the trespassers; they cannot believe their eyes: Six thousand trees. Eighteen thousand nails.

Your house lit up in the distance, blue, red, white. The church with its quieter light somewhere opposite. Empty. The woods full of silence and iron. Your face slowly drying. P.'s boots digging up the dirt beside you. Full night now. The first stars. Touching their cold holes into the sky.

At the gate of the garden a hand stops you. You let it. The same officer who brought you from the Moores' to the station, eyes gleaming when he sees you. Erik on the garden step, flanked by two men. He is not allowed to touch you. A breeze through the lettuce, the long tubes of rhubarb, the bent heads of the sunflowers. You step inside the house.

———

Did you hear the truck this morning. Yes. Did you hear the saw. Yes. Did you hear a scream, a sound, what came after. Silence. Did you know he was coming. Yes. Were you worried about him coming. Yes. Why. Because I knew what he wanted. What did he want. To kill them. To kill who. The trees. And that bothered you? Yes. You spend a lot of time in the woods. Yes. So what did you do. Silence. Xie. What did you do.

You don't look at the man gripping your elbow. The door to the attic in pieces on the carpet. Brass lock twisted, sparkling, between two planks of white wood. Such noise overhead. Stranger after stranger walking the stairs up into your room. You count the steps to the bed. Hear the whisper of the sheet pulled from bone. Your lamb. A shout. Don't think. About the body in someone else's arms, someone who does not love it, who does not know it can be loved. You look at your father. He looks only at you. Boots on the ladder. All the silver from the closet carried down in pieces. The cape. The skirt. The crown. Even you do not understand it. The body in a bag on the floor, the zipper closing its teeth so tight together. Remember. When you brought him here. The gold filling the room to the ceiling. They put you on your knees as they carry the body out. You sob and sob. It will go back to the church, behind thicker glass, a more solid lock, more beautiful because you have adored it. P. lays his cheek against the back of your skull. Shh. In the garden, in the woods, on the Moores' farm, in your bed, you made as much life as you could. You looked for it every-where, even in the body, even in bone, because this is how you see the world: as desperately, infinitely living. All you wanted was to help it. Go on. For a little while longer. Someone holds your wrists behind your back, pushes your head down so that you must look at the floor, which is wood, beneath which is dirt, and beneath that, stone: and farther still, beneath every road, every path, there is fire. It is a mistake to think of the soul as something dark: there is light spread over all the earth, isn't there? You, at least, have seen it. You see it now. Pulled to your feet. Walking from one imperfect place to another. The trees, alive, behind you.

ACKNOWLEDGMENTS

Thanks to:
Danielle Meijer, Meredith Kaffel Simonoff, Emily Bell,
Javier Ramirez, H. Peter Steeves, Jackson Howard, Na
Kim, Chloe Texier-Rose, Catherine Lacey, Daniel Kraus,
Kathe Koja, William and Charlotte Nickell, Bonnie, Xiu
Xiu, Alexander McQueen, P., and the lovers and the de-
fenders of nature in all her forms.